Centurion Comes Home

SHOWELL STYLES

FABER AND FABER

London   Boston

First published in 1980
by Faber and Faber Limited
3 Queen Square London WC1N 3AU
Photoset in Great Britain by
Granada Graphics Mitcham
Printed by Lowe and Brydone Printers Limited
Thetford Norfolk
All rights reserved

British Library Cataloguing in Publication Data

Styles, Showell
Centurion comes home.
I. Title
823'.9' IF   PR6037.T96C/
ISBN 0-571-11610-8

AUTHOR'S NOTE

All the chief characters in this story actually existed. All the main events actually happened.

Prologue, June 1744

The Lord Chancellor of England damned and con-founded indiscriminately as his horse bucketed down the uneven slope of turf. Remembering the groom who rode a few yards behind him he restrained his language and shouted instead after the rider cantering ahead of him, half-seen in the white early-morning mist that lay across Gilkicker Down.

"Elizabeth! Not so fast!"

The girl on the bay horse raised an arm in answer but held on at the same pace. Lord Hardwicke reined his mount to a trot, the groom doing likewise to keep his distance, and adjusted his wig and hat to the accompani-ment of inarticulate growls. He was a man who liked all things done with regularity and order and he had had no breakfast. Since he was also a very just man he told himself it was his own fault. He doted on his daughter, spoiled her; though that was no reason why he should allow Elizabeth to get him out of bed before sunrise on a June morning and make him ride seven miles on the offchance of seeing a ship.

The white mist was brightening and thinning every moment, though it still hid Spithead and the Island three miles away across the strait. The dew sparkled on the grass and Lord Hardwicke's spirits began to rise despite his empty belly. He could reasonably blame Chance for his present discomforts, he reflected as he trotted on

CENTRAL

downhill towards the shore. The First Lord had invited the Lord Chancellor and his daughter the Lady Elizabeth Yorke to spend a few days with him in Hampshire, and it was mere chance that they had been at Cams Hall last night when the sloop captain had called to acquaint Sir Charles Wager that he had sighted *Centurion* off the Start on the previous day. And of course Elizabeth—

Lord Hardwicke's heavy brows drew together as he considered Elizabeth. She had met George Anson perhaps four times in all and there was no doubt that she had been much taken with him, somewhat to her father's dismay. Anson was a first-rate sea officer with an admirable record, but there were some things about him which Lord Hardwicke, a stern judge of men and modes, had found less than admirable; in addition to the fact that Anson was old enough to be Elizabeth's father. That had been nearly four years ago, and here was Elizabeth rushing to get a first glimpse of Anson's ship after his long absence. The Lord Chancellor shifted uneasily in his saddle. He knew himself for a man of rare ability and there was his massive reform of English equity jurisdiction to prove it, but he doubted his competence to deal with a wayward daughter.

Elizabeth was waiting for him where the turf of the Down ended in a miniature cliff with the pebble beach just below it. Characteristically, she had dismounted without waiting for the groom and had taken off her feathered tricorne hat. The little wind of morning fluttered the long skirt of her plum-coloured habit and twitched at the queue of dark hair tied with a bow that matched the habit. Lord Hardwicke drew rein and the groom sprang down to hold his stirrup.

"Your speed was injudicious, miss," reproved the Lord Chancellor as he lowered his heavy body from the saddle. "In this mist you might have galloped yourself into the Channel."

"But I didn't, Father."

She turned a smiling face to him. It was a face neither beautiful nor ugly, but not to be called plain. The brilliance of the brown eyes under level dark brows offset the hint of oddity that came of a nose too long, lips too full, and a smooth and lofty brow. The tight riding-coat with its huge lapels showed her figure much too slim to be fashionable.

"That was your good fortune," grunted Lord Hardwicke. "Take the horses, Benson."

"I'm always fortunate," said Elizabeth. "My face isn't my fortune, so that's merely just."

They strolled slowly along the turf edge above the beach. The mist had retreated beyond the small waves that broke on the pebbles and the pearly waters of Spithead glinted as the sun began to struggle through the vapours.

"Fortune won't bring *Centurion* into Spithead for you to see at this precise moment," Lord Hardwicke said irritably. "It's odds she's either in Portsmouth Harbour already or hours away south of the Wight. I warn you, Elizabeth, I'm not going to dawdle here for more than thirty minutes."

"One hour, Father." The girl slipped her arm through his. "It's odds—since you're in a betting mood—that she'll pass within an hour."

"Ridiculous."

"Not at all." She squeezed his arm. "I'm your daughter, therefore I'm clever. Observe. Captain Tooley told us last night that *Centurion* was off the Start at five o'clock on the morning of the thirteenth. That's a trifle under fifty leagues from Gilkicker Point. This light westerly has held steady for the past two days and *Centurion*'s a slow sailer—three knots, Tooley thought she'd make of it. Fifty leagues at three knots. Surely the Lord High Chancellor can work a sum?"

Her father smiled and wagged his head. "I leave arithmetic to my clerks."

"Very lax of you, my lord. Well, the answer is fifty hours. Today is the fifteenth and the fiftieth hour expired a few minutes ago." She did not conceal her excitement.

9

"If only the mist would lift! *Centurion* should have entered Spithead by now."

"I trust she has. My breakfast, it appears, depends upon her adherence to my lady's programme."

They walked on for a short distance, Elizabeth's gaze continually on the receding mists to seaward, and then turned back. Hazy sunlight illuminated the green slopes, and beyond Benson and the horses the grey stone of Gilkicker Fort stood clear. A puff of white broke from the walls of the fort and the boom of a cannon followed. Elizabeth seized her father's arm and swung him round to face the sea.

"Look!"

It was a breath rather than a word. Scarcely a mile away across the glimmering water a great ship had appeared, stealing like a wraith through a veil of mist, with all sail set to the topgallants. Her brown flank with its double row of gunports was towards them and a small white cloud jetted from it as she answered the fort's guns, which continued to bang away in completion of the eleven-gun salute to the commodore's broad pendant at *Centurion*'s mainmast-head.

"So you were right about *Centurion*," said the Lord Chancellor between the cannon-booms. "I doubt whether you are right about her captain."

Elizabeth answered without taking her gaze from the ship. "He's brought her safely home in spite of all."

Some account of *Centurion*'s adventures in the Pacific had been brought to England a year ago, and the tale had been a harrowing one.

"He has." Lord Hardwicke nodded slowly. "His career and fortune are assured. And I fancy that is all Mr Anson cares about, my dear."

The ship, moving slowly onward through the mist-wreaths, was furling her main courses as she approached the harbour entrance out of sight beyond the point. The girl was silent until the high poop had vanished behind the jut of land.

"You thought him the man for your purpose once, my lord," she said then, quietly.

"For England's purpose," he corrected her. "England's need was never greater. We are at war with France since March, and this will be the conclusive struggle for power in Europe. Though it should last for ten, twenty, or fifty years the final triumph—depend upon it—will be his who has the strongest Navy. You've heard Sir Charles talk of our present state. Ships few, old, manned by a rabble, administered by politicians and place-seekers. Not one strong man, one disinterested man, at Admiralty."

"Sir Charles," began the girl.

"The First Lord is long past eighty, Elizabeth. We cannot expect him to raise the storm which a cry of 'Reform the Navy' would bring about his ears. No. What is needed is a strong man in his prime, a master of ships and men and the sea, caring more for the Navy's future than for his own—but pho, pho, pho!" Lord Hardwicke interrupted himself abruptly. "You and I need breakfast, not an oration. Come."

They began to walk towards the horses, the warmth of the climbing sun on their backs. Lord Hardwicke's broad brow was still furrowed with thought.

"A man in a million," he said, half to himself. "And George Anson's no different from a hundred others of his profession. A good sea-captain with a chance of reaching admiral's rank—and that, with cards and wine and women, is all his interest." He darted a glance at the girl walking beside him. "You thought him more than that?"

Elizabeth considered for a moment. "I thought him capable of much more if there was something he really wanted. It would be wise to suspend judgement, Father. After all, it's long since we last saw Mr Anson."

"H'm. Four years, I apprehend."

"Three years, nine months, and six days," said his daughter. "Since *Centurion* departed for the South Seas, that is. She sailed on September 20th."

11

"You're very ready with calculations this morning. Very well, Benson. Assist my lady."

The groom helped Elizabeth into the awkward side-saddle and hurried to hold Lord Hardwicke's stirrup.

"And that was nearly three months later than she was ordered," added the Lord Chancellor when he had mounted; the prospect of breakfast in half-an-hour had lightened his mood. "My learned companion was not aware of that, I fancy."

"Indeed I wasn't," smiled Elizabeth, setting the bay in motion.

"Small wonder," grunted her father as they began to ride up the gentle slope of Gilkicker Down. "It was kept a close secret. That sailing date was known only to five persons—myself and the other Lords Justices who signed the order, and Mr Anson, the Commodore of the squadron. It was the thirtieth of June."

ONE

The Hand of Fortune

1

"The thirtieth of June," said Kitty Clive slowly. "So you'll sail six days from now, George, for t'other side the world. And God only knows if I'll ever see you again."

Mr George Anson, who was buttoning his breeches with his back to the woman on the bed, silently cursed his unwariness in naming that date; he was not a babbler, but in the Nirvana after a love-making his tongue was apt to wag—as he ought to know by now.

"It's the fate of every seaman and his mistress, my dear," he said aloud, lightly.

He could see her reflected in the tall mirror in front of him. The dull yellow light from a candle-branch on the wall gilded her voluptuous nakedness as she lay sprawled among the tumbled sheets, but the shadow of the bed-canopy fell across her face and hid its expression. It was just four months, he recalled, since he had first seen her at Vauxhall where she was singing in Mr Handel's *Berenice*. He had joined the circle of congratulatory beaux after the performance and she had chosen him to escort her chair to her house in Russell Street. George Anson had never known a more enchanting mistress. Whenever he could spare time from the arduous work at Portsmouth to come up to London, he had spent his nights with her in this room.

Kitty pulled a fold of sheet across her thighs. "You leave London today?"

13

"Tomorrow," he told her briskly. "I ride post for Portsmouth at daybreak."

"You'll be away for two years, perhaps three," she said in a low voice. "Yet you waited until—until an hour ago to tell me."

Mr Anson, intent on the adjustment of the frilled lace at his throat, answered her coolly.

"It slipped my memory, Kitty. I'm much pressed with affairs lately."

He took his tie-wig from the table by the mirror and settled it carefully on his close-cropped head with the aid of the glass. The face that confronted him in the mirror showed few lines of age or care considering he was forty-three, but the wide firm mouth and level brows, no less than the uncompromising jut of nose and chin, revealed a man mature and accustomed to command, assured to the point of self-confidence. The morning light filtering through the closed curtains at the window struck a glint of blue from a pair of deep-set eyes narrowed by years of gazing at sea horizons. Mr Anson surveyed his reflection with satisfaction as he donned a long yellow waistcoat brocaded with orange, and slung on the baldric for his small-sword. Kitty watched him in silence, her face in shadow.

"And what am I to do," she said at last, in a voice devoid of expression, "while you're away for two years and more?"

"Why, Kitty my dear, I'm no coxcomb, I hope." Mr Anson was shrugging himself into an orange-satin coat as he spoke. "You'll console yourself, I don't doubt. You've no lack of admirers and most of 'em are gentlemen. Daintree, Lord Carless, Everdon—but I'd except Peter O'Hara. I've heard, never mind how, that O'Hara is suspect of disaffection towards King George, which makes him no fit friend for Mrs Clive."

Kitty made no reply to this. Anson, bending to fasten his small-sword to the baldric, did not observe the tight clenching of her fists.

14

"There'll be no women for me this voyage," he went on. "I'm made Commodore of a squadron and that means my ships are my mistresses." He came to the bedside and stood looking down at her. "But mark this, Kitty. What you do while I'm gone makes no difference to my offer. I asked you to marry me six weeks ago and you said you'd consider it. I shall ask you again when I return, and it's odd but I'll have more to offer. I'll be Rear-Admiral Anson, as like as not. You'll not forget that, Kitty?"

"I'll not forget," she said in a whisper.

Anson knelt, not ungracefully, and pressed his lips to her hand. "Then it's *au revoir*, my dear."

He stood up, took his hat from a stool by the door, and went out of the bedroom without a backward glance. The landing outside was gloomy, for it was not yet six o'clock and the Russell Street house faced north. At the foot of the stairs Ham, his Negro servant, was curled up snoring on a pile of blankets. Mr Anson woke him with a well-placed kick and bade him show a leg and look lively, whereat Ham uncoiled his six-and-a-half feet in a single lithe movement and followed his master into the street.

The morning air was cool and free as yet from the dust and stink of London in midsummer, though it bore a not unpleasing odour of flower-scent mingled with the smell of green vegetables. No chair-men were about at that hour and in any case Mr Anson's lodging in Killick Street off the Strand was no more than fifteen minutes' walk away. With Ham, in dark-blue coat and breeches, ambling loose-limbed at his heels he emerged at the end of Russell Street into the precursory bustle of the Market and steered an unfaltering course across its littered cobbles between sweating porters, shouting barrow-men, and half-erected wooden stalls. Beyond Henrietta Street the hubbub of Covent Garden was left behind and he could walk more freely, his slightly rolling stride at variance with his satin coat and high-heeled shoes. As he walked he hummed one of Mr Handel's airs, a minuet from *Berenice*. Mr Anson was well pleased with himself, and (he would

15

have declared) with reason.

Thirty years in His Majesty's Navy, which for most of that time had been engaged in desultory warfare against Spain, had left George Anson with enough Spanish to read Cervantes; and his favourite saying of Sancho Panza was "When they bring you the heifer be ready with the rope." To be born fortunate, as he believed himself to be, was only half an advantage; the man himself must be alert to seize each lucky chance and wrest it to his own desire. Thus it had been Fortune who on his promotion to captain's rank had given him *Centurion*, a sound ship instead of one of the score of decrepit 60-gun warships, ill-rigged and half-rotten, maintained by an improvident Admiralty. But it had been Anson who had drilled and flogged her crew until she was the efficient fighting-ship he wanted to assist his rise in his profession. Fortune, no doubt, had provided those two earlier defensive cruises off the South Carolina coast, with their spells ashore in Georgetown and Charleston in the society of wealthy planters; but it had been Anson's skill at whist that had won him the money to purchase 12,000 Carolina acres, an estate which still brought him a considerable income. And Fortune had decreed the renewal of war with Spain a few weeks before *Centurion*'s return from Barbados, her captain the very man to command the daring expedition then being planned to harass the Spanish possessions overseas. As he had hinted to Kitty Clive, George Anson—appointed Commander-in-Chief with the rank of Commodore—had no doubt of his ability to reap further promotion from this command.

Master and servant emerged into the Strand and hazy sunlight. The mists were lifting from the river and the stink of Thames was in their nostrils, raw reality after the perfumed Elysium of the bedroom in Russell Street. Kitty Clive, reflected Mr Anson, was another instance of his genius assisting his good fortune. Among the arts his one passion was music; and Kitty, beside being an accomplished mistress, possessed the finest soprano voice he had ever heard. It would be both delightful and convenient to have her as his wife—his proposal had been perfectly serious—and her undoubtedly easy virtue (if it remained firmly in the past after marriage) could be no drawback when so many men of consequence were wedding singers and actresses no more chaste than themselves. He let his thoughts dwell on last night's ecstasies and felt a momentary regret that there would be no more for a year or two. But here he was at the door of his lodging in Killick Street and the hired footman was opening it. The man handed him a sealed note as he stepped inside.

"This came last night, sir, by messenger. After you'd gorn out."

Mr Anson opened it and read that Lord Hardwicke would be obliged if the Commodore would call at his house in Downing Street at ten that morning. It was satisfactory to be given his naval rank; more satisfactory to be able to oblige the Lord Chancellor of England.

"Coffee and hot bread, Ham, double-quick," said George Anson; and forgot Kitty Clive in his need for breakfast.

His complacency would not have survived knowledge of Mrs Clive's activities at that moment.

For a breathing-space after the door of the Russell Street house had closed behind her departing lover Kitty had remained lying on the bed, tense and motionless. Then, springing up and wrapping a bedgown about her nakedness, she began to pace rapidly up and down the room. Her long brown hair floated behind her and her eyes flashed with the increasing fury of her thoughts. Kitty Clive could swear as freely as any fashionable lady, but this morning her feelings were beyond relief by the spouting of oaths. The heartless brute! The beef-witted, blockish numskull! One or both he was in his treatment of her. And to think she had found him attractive, lavished affection on him! Well, this morning he had killed affection with two savage blows, the more cruel in that he had been unaware of their cruelty. To reveal, in the careless aftermath of a night of love, that he was going away at once, leaving her for two years and more! Did he expect her to accept that as casually as he mentioned it? The man was a cold fish after all, with no thought beyond his own appetites and ambitions. And then—the crowning insult which had left her breathless with rage and lit the slow-match for her explosion of hatred.

Anson was by no means Mrs Clive's first lover but she had always had her own sort of chastity, kept her own pride. Her favours were reserved for the man who could excite in her something more than lust, something of liking and real affection. There had not been many such. But he—he had dealt with her as if her own feelings were of no account. As if she were a whore to be bought and sold or passed from one master to another. He would marry her when he came back, would he? Take her up again from the arms of one of his nominees. *"Daintree, Lord Carless, Everdon–"* His voice echoed hatefully in her ears. *"But I'd except Peter O'Hara."* O generous, to leave her the choice of three!

She halted suddenly in her pacing, trembling with the intensity of whipped-up passion. She needed a means of retaliation and he had left her none, for he would be gone from London tomorrow. Gone on this precious Expedition to harry the Spaniards in the Pacific. He had flaunted it before her, disclosing how much more important it was to him than she was. And there was a way, a possible way, of striking back at him through that.

Kitty checked the furious surge of her thoughts, but only for a moment. Hate and anger might dismount later on, but now they were riding her blindly. *The thirtieth of June.* She had been sharp enough to notice his concern that she had remembered that. And there was Peter O'Hara. George had heard that Peter was "suspect of disaffection towards King George" and Kitty Clive knew rather more of him than that. He had never been her lover but she had a liking for him, a handsome Ishmael at odds with Authority and moving amid dark rumours and mysteries. To a very few, and Kitty was one, it was known that Peter O'Hara had a Spanish mother. And Kitty knew, too, where she could find him. In a voice very unlike the dulcet soprano that so pleased Mr Anson she shouted for her maid to come at once and help her get dressed.

2

By a judicious combination of patience and thrashing George Anson had made Ham into an admirable servant. The Negro had been won at cards from the owner of a Carolina plantation; and since his new master's cane was an altogether lighter matter than the overseer's whip the thrashings had encouraged rather than subdued Ham's devotion to Anson. He had been Captain's Servant, afloat and ashore, for five years now and in either circumstance there was little left for him to learn. He shaved his master after breakfast on the morning of June 24th and then was bidden to pack their belongings for the journey to Portsmouth on the morrow. Anson, who was impatient to return to his squadron, was to ride post while Ham followed by the slower stage-coach with their main baggage. This being ordered, Anson called for hat and sword.

"And get me a sedan," he added. *"Vaya rapido!"*

"Yassah," said Ham with a flash of teeth like marble tombstones, and sprang to obey.

Mr Anson stepped out of his glass-panelled chair opposite the house in Downing Street a little before ten o'clock. He paid his fee to the front chair-man (characteristically, without a glance at the man or notice of his thanks) and mounted the three steps to the Lord Chancellor's door. He was no stranger here. Lord Hardwicke was one of the four Lords Justices, deputies of His Majesty King George II, who had signed the orders that reposed in an inner pocket of Anson's wide-skirted coat, and Anson had conferred with him on several previous occasions; the other three were the Prime Minister, the First Lord of the Admiralty, and the Duke of Newcastle, none of whom had he so far set eyes on. The earlier visits had made him acquainted with the Lord Chancellor's daughter, Lady Elizabeth Yorke, a gawky, odd-looking girl in her early twenties. A footman in powder and livery opened to his knock and took his hat and sword, and a second footman, with much bowing and gesturing, ushered him up the wide stairway and into the Lord Chancellor's study.

Lord Hardwicke, a big man with a heavy jowl and very keen grey eyes, stood up from his chair at a desk and exchanged bows with his visitor.

"Pray be seated, Mr Anson. You are punctual."

"Few men would be otherwise when your lordship names the hour."

"You think so?" Lord Hardwicke's glance was sardonic. "Punctuality is a *sine qua non* with your ship's officers, no doubt. With His Majesty's ministers it's a virtue *in nubibus*—as you must be aware by now. Your original orders, signed by the King's own hand, were dated in January, were they not?"

"The thirty-first of that month, my lord."

"Just so. Then the expedition plans were changed and you were given new orders. It's now the end of June. Are your six vessels ready for sea?"

"I shall sail on the thirtieth as ordered, my lord."

The Chancellor frowned. "You've not answered my question, Mr Anson. I know, for I am in close touch with the First Lord, of your efforts to man your ships and the opposition you've encountered in every quarter. I know that instead of the five hundred troops required by the King's instructions you've been given ninety-eight marines. I know—don't interrupt me, pray—that you're here in London, when your presence is urgently needed at Portsmouth, to appeal to the Admiralty for help."

"I left Captain Norris of the *Gloucester* in charge," said Anson quickly. "I've every confidence—"

"Confound it, man, I'm not censuring you!" broke in Hardwicke brusquely. "Your endeavours deserve nothing but praise, successful or no. What I ask you is this. Do you seriously consider your force, diminished as it is, strong enough to make a perilous ocean voyage of eight or nine thousand miles and, at the end of it, wage war against the empire of Spain?"

Mr Anson took his time to answer this. "In its present state," he said at length, "the squadron's unfit to wage war against anything. In six or eight months—it may well be that long before I'm in the Pacific—I'll guarantee to have a fighting squadron strong enough to fulfil His Majesty's purpose."

"Indeed."

The Chancellor pursed his lips, scowled, and picked up a paper from the desk.

"I have this from the First Lord. Sir Charles informs me that the Admiral at Spithead has obeyed his order and collected every available man for transfer to your ships. Thirty-seven men and boys have been sent from the *Salisbury* merchant vessel and thirty-two from the Portsmouth hospital." He put the paper down and slammed his hand upon it. "And these fine fellows are to be added to your ships' companies—half of which, as I'm told, are gaolbirds and pressed men as it is. Will you still maintain, sir, that you've seamen enough to take your ships to sea on the thirtieth?"

"On the lower deck of a man-of-war, my lord," replied Anson composedly, "every gaolbird and pressed man is a hand, from the moment he comes aboard. He can haul on a rope with a score of others, hoist the sails, get the ship to sea. After that"—he shrugged his shoulders—"he lives or he dies. If he lives, it's because he's become a seaman."

Lord Hardwicke grunted and rubbed his chin, frowning. He seemed about to speak, thought better of it, and continued to rub his chin. Anson saw this indecision with surprise; it was unlike the Chancellor's customary forthright precision. To bridge the silence he spoke again.

21

"As to my endeavours in London, they've not been entirely unsuccessful. The First Lord has promised to approach the military authorities immediately with a demand for five hundred troops. There's yet time—"

"Sir Charles Wager approached *me*, Mr Anson. He's an old friend, my late wife's cousin indeed, but I tell you frankly he's too old and stupid to take issue with men like Walpole and Newcastle."

Hardwicke set both hands on the edge of his desk and directed a steady stare at the man before him. His deep voice, uncertain at first, gathered strength as he spoke.

"Mr Anson, I requested this meeting because—well, for two reasons. The first, to ensure that you apprehend your instructions, is mere formality. The second is to offer you an apology and an explanation. The latter, I fancy, should precede the former. I believe you concern yourself very little with politics?"

"As little as possible, my lord. I'm a sea officer in His Majesty's Navy and I concern myself with my duty."

"Very creditable," grunted the Chancellor drily. "Yet politics greatly concern the Navy just now. Too much so, indeed. The delay of this Expedition, the senseless chopping and changing of plan, the frustrations and hindrances—all politics, Mr Anson. I presume you're aware that the King and his Prime Minister are at variance over the present war?"

The question was rhetorical. Anson inclined his head.

"The rest follows, then. Sir Robert detests this war with Spain and hates the very idea of the Expedition. The King and the people demand it, and they too have powerful supporters. In the result we have intrigues, cabals, factions, and all from the highest to the lowest in power resolved to do nothing until they see which way the cat will jump. That should explain, if explanation is needed, the obstruction you have met with. Now for my apology, which I shall make *brevi manu*."

He paused as if to marshal his words and Anson leaned forward, frowning slightly.

"From a man in your lordship's position," he began, "an apology—"

"Is in this case necessary for my conscience's sake," Hardwicke cut him short. "Sir Charles Wager passed to me your urgent request for the five hundred troops specified in His Majesty's instructions. It was useless to approach the military authorities. I went straight to the Duke and told him you would resign your command of the Expedition unless they were sent to Portsmouth immediately. Newcastle hummed and ha'd but he signed the order there and then. By now your five hundred are on their way to Portsmouth." There was a hint of defiance in his stare. "Well? Have you no comment, sir?"

Anson met his gaze frankly. "The end justified the means, my lord. Pray accept my thanks. I'm profoundly relieved."

"I'm glad of it. I take it that you have in fact entertained no idea of resignation?"

"No, my lord."

Hardwicke pushed his fingers under his wig to scratch his head. "Um. You're a patient man, Mr Anson. Do you never feel impatience with the incompetence of your superiors? With the intolerable muddle—I'm candid with you—of the Admiralty, the mismanagement of ships and men?"

"If I do, my lord, I repress it," returned Anson with a faint smile. "I've been fourteen years in command of King's ships and I've learned to expect—since we're being candid—no more from Admiralty than just that."

"Your ship's company expect more than that from you, sir," Hardwicke shot at him, "or *Centurion* would have been at the sea-bottom long since. Would you not welcome the chance to take order with these clerks and jacks-in-office, mould efficiency out of potential chaos as you've done with your ships?"

Anson's smile broadened and suddenly he laughed. "Your pardon, my lord. I was picturing my first lieutenant and a boatswain's mate armed with cat-o'-nine-tails

23

disciplining the Admiralty. The task is not for me. It's not my province."

"It was not my province, Mr Anson, to interfere with military matters in the acquiring of your troops," said the Lord Chancellor severely.

Considering himself reproved without cause, Anson held his tongue. Lord Hardwicke too was silent for a moment, pursuing his own thoughts. He was a statesman and looked to the future. In the present he saw the Board of Admiralty rotten with idlers and place-seekers; the First Lord, Charles Wager, over eighty and senile before his time; no man of resolution and integrity to bring sorely-needed reform to the Navy. He had visualised Anson as filling that vital role in the years to come. If this Expedition ended in success Anson would be a national hero, receive rapid promotion and the King's favour, stand at the threshold of political power. If he set naval reform for his objective he would have every chance of achieving it. But here were two "ifs", and the Expedition's success was one of them. It was a precarious adventure at best and might well end in abject failure. Lord Hardwicke sighed and returned to the present.

"Well, let's to business," he said with a glance at the clock on the overmantel. "I am bidden to bring you to the withdrawing-room at eleven, to take tea with my daughter and her aunt, Lady Crosby."

"That will be both honour and pleasure," said Anson.

Hardwicke's grim mouth curved in a smile. "I wish you may find it so. Elizabeth, I believe, proposes to catechise you concerning the domestic arrangements in His Majesty's ships of war."

"The catechism, my lord, was begun at my last visit," said Anson with an answering smile.

"You must excuse her. She has an inquiring mind. And now—you have the orders and instructions with you?"

Anson laid the documents on the desk and drew his chair nearer. He had his orders by heart and there could be little to discuss at this late stage. To the original

"Instructions for our trusty and well-beloved George Anson Esq." headed by the Royal signature were appended the later instructions of the Lords Justices. In sum, he was to sail in *Centurion* as Commodore of a squadron of six warships which also included the *Gloucester* and *Severn* of 50 guns, the *Pearl* of 40 guns, *Wager* of 28 and the sloop *Tryal* of 8 guns. He was to proceed by way of the Cape Verde Islands and Cape Horn into the Pacific and cruise off the Spanish coast of South America, where the business of his mission began. *"You are to use your best endeavours to annoy and distress the Spaniards, either at sea or land, to the utmost of your power, by taking, sinking, burning, or otherwise destroying all their ships and vessels,"* ran the wording (in which, Anson thought, some lawyer less concise than Lord Hardwicke must have had a hand) and added that the land-forces he would take with him were to be used *"to seize, surprise, or take any of the towns or places belonging to the Spaniards on the coast, that you may judge worthy of making such an enterprize upon."* Finally, he was to look out for the Spanish galleon which every year made the voyage from Acapulco to Manila laden with treasure; after which he might complete a circumnavigation of the globe by returning home *"by the way of China, which you are authorised to do, or by way of Cape Horn, as you shall think best for our service, and for the preservation of the ships and the men on board them."*

It was upon this last clause that the Lord Chancellor, when he had skimmed rapidly through the orders with a forefinger on the carefully scripted lines, made his only comment.

"If you make but the one passage round the Horn, Mr Anson," he remarked, "you will be the fourteenth seaman to encircle the world, or so I am informed."

"And the seventh Englishman, my lord. Francis Drake was the first."

"Ah, you've studied the matter, I see." Lord Hardwicke rose to his feet. "I wish you Drake's fortune in the taking of treasure but I'll be better pleased to see you and your

25

ships safe home again."

Anson stood up, smiling. "I hope to fulfil your lordship's expectations on both accounts. I was born fortunate."

"You must tell Lady Elizabeth that. She makes the same claim."

They left the study and came by way of a gallery hung with portraits of kings and statesmen to a lofty room with a moulded ceiling, and wallpaper in the Chinese taste. There was a spinet in one corner and a tall window framed distant trees in St James's Park. Mr Anson made his bows to Lady Crosby, a plump dowager with a towering coiffure like a mountain of snow, and Lady Elizabeth Yorke, who turned from discussion of some half-completed embroidery on a frame in the window embrasure. Elizabeth's thin figure was clothed in a morning gown of flowered cotton and her dark brown hair, unpowdered, was crowned with a little cap of white lace.

"You're five minutes late, Philip," Lady Crosby chattered, tugging at a silken bell-pull. "I vow you men have no conception of the flight of time. Here's two poor creatures dying for a dish of tea—Mr Anson, a chair here. We are to bid you Godspeed, I hear, but let's not be sad. We shall see you return the conquering hero, I vow and declare. The South Seas, is it not? Lord Clanricard was telling me the islands are paradisal. Shall you go ashore upon them, to pluck bananas and coconuts? In Lord Clanricard's view, the climate—"

Anson breasted the flood with smiles and monosyllables until a footman entered with teapot and china cups on a silver tray. Lady Crosby dispensed tea with hardly a pause in her discourse. Anson, sipping a beverage he privately disliked, noted the covert interchange between Lord Hardwicke and his daughter, a whimsical shrug from the Lord Chancellor and a little answering smile from Elizabeth. The smile brought animation to her odd face, giving it a quaint attractiveness. He recalled Kitty Clive's opulent charms and rare beauty and thought there could hardly be two women more unlike in face and form.

Over the second cup Lady Crosby interrupted her account of the habits of savage Indians (as instanced by Lord Clanricard) to address her brother-in-law.

"While I remember it, Philip, I must have your advice on my embroidery. It's the Yorke crest I'm working, as you know." She turned to Anson. "An old family, sir. I believe the Ansons of Shugborough may claim antiquity, too."

"Yeoman stock, ma'am, until my great-grandfather made his fortune under the first James. We are Staffordshire folk—"

"Ah, yes. And your uncle Thomas is Lord Macclesfield, as we know." Lady Crosby set down her empty cup. "You'll take more tea? No? Then Philip, I require your opinion on the placing of the Yorke motto in my design. The scroll takes up far too much room. I vow it's the greatest nuisance. And my gold thread, which the Duchess of Bedford gave me—"

Still talking, she drew the Lord Chancellor away into the window embrasure. Mr Anson, wondering whether to suspect a matchmaking manoeuvre, was secretly amused. Hardwicke's daughter? Why, he was twice her age. He shifted his chair politely so as to face Elizabeth, who sat demurely upright in an armchair at his side.

"I protest your ladyship blooms more charmingly each time we meet," he began according to form.

"Thank you, sir," she said quickly. "But shall we dispense with fashionable affectations? I believe you despise them as much as I do, and time is short. Our conversation was uncompleted last time, if you remember."

Anson laughed. "Indeed I do. I was not sorry to escape from your denunciation of the cat-o'-nine-tails."

"You ran from an opponent of greater force." Elizabeth's smile was short-lived. "I still maintain that lashing with the cat should be unnecessary in His

Majesty's ships."

"Should be—there I can agree with your ladyship. But I deal with matters as they are, not as they should be. I assure you that the lash is very necessary at present."

"Commodore Anson should look beyond the present," she told him, and wriggled her shoulders impatiently. "We waste time. I must tell you I'm better informed on Navy matters than I was. I cajoled Sir Charles into procuring me a visit on board the *Grafton*, sixty guns, newly returned from the Biscay patrol and lying off Deptford at moorings. I learned a great deal from that visit."

"Including some nautical lingo, I perceive."

She ignored that. "I made Captain Rogers show me the whole of his ship from top to bottom and answer all my questions. I fear I was keeping him from his duty, for he became a little irritable, but he was helpful."

Anson's sympathy went out to Captain Rogers. "May I ask why your ladyship takes such interest in a ship of war?" he asked curiously.

"Because my interest has always been in our Navy, sir, and because I'm my father's daughter." Elizabeth glanced at the pair stooping above the embroidery-frame in the window. "Lord Hardwicke has long preached the urgent need for a strong Navy if our country is to survive in years to come, and I was his first convert. Mr Anson, no nation can possess a strong Navy while she treats her seamen as we treat ours—as lower than beasts and of less account than flies."

"Your ladyship exaggerates," said Anson, frowning. "The facts are that the lower deck—"

"The facts I have seen for myself," she interrupted firmly. "Four hundred men are packed into a space less than this house affords, away from light and air, crawling with vermin, there to live for months—years, sometimes. My horses at home are better housed. My dogs are better fed."

"The accommodation in a ship is fixed as is the number

28

of men to man her." he told her tolerantly. "You and I couldn't exist in such conditions, but they're no worse than such fellows live in ashore."

"They should be better for men in the King's service!" she cried—quite angrily, he noticed with some surprise. "And the meanest beggar in London has more freedom than one of those four hundred. Captain Rogers may be a humane man—I believe he is—but he has all the power of the cruellest tyrant if he chose to exercise it. Power to judge and condemn at his sole discretion. Power to flog, and torture, and hang."

"And he needs that power," said Anson sharply. "Without it his ship couldn't keep the sea, much less fight the King's enemies."

He was a little astonished to find himself arguing as with another man. She was, after all, a mere girl, though an oddly unfeminine one. He moderated his tone.

"Your ladyship doesn't regard the full picture. The bulk of a ship's crew are indeed no better than beasts when they're taken abroad. They fear nothing but the lash for punishment, love nothing but rum for reward. I've seen it often and I know. I'll make half of them into seamen and the other half will remain beasts, needed still for the hard work a beast can do. You waste your pity."

Elizabeth's brown eyes widened and flashed and for an instant he thought she would lose her temper. She controlled herself quickly, however, and shook her head at him with a wry smile.

"I think you are unjust, Mr Anson, to yourself as well as your men," she said. "I don't waste my pity but my time. For it seems you're well satisfied with the Navy and see no need for improvement."

"That is far from the case," he replied seriously. "No sea-officer could say that, with the Fleet in its present state. Two-thirds of our ships of the line are out of service, most of them so rotten as to be beyond repair. There should be new ships building, the worthless hulks should be broken up—"

He checked himself. This was a topic for a wardroom, not for a lady's withdrawing-room. But Elizabeth was regarding him with approval.

"There we are agreed, at least," she said. "Reform at the highest levels is sadly overdue. But, sir—your new ships will be but wooden shells. Whether they can beat the Spaniards—or the French, at need—depends on the men in them."

The debate over the embroidery-frame was plainly drawing to an end. The girl leaned forward urgently, her quaint-featured face so close to Anson's that he could see his reflection in the pupils of those persuasive brown eyes.

"I wish you well on your voyage, Mr Anson," she said hurriedly in a low voice. "And I wish you'll remember God's truth—that no man in your crew is a mere beast. The lowest can feel pride in the Service, the meanest can be given self-respect, if they're treated as men. That is your way to a strong Navy. When *Centurion* comes home—"

She stopped abruptly. Lord Hardwicke and his sister-in-law were coming towards them from the window. Lady Crosby patted Anson's arm as he rose from his chair.

"Alack, we intrude upon confidences, I fear," she said archly. "But Philip must needs return to his study. It's ridiculous, I declare, that a Lord Chancellor should have so little leisure."

"The King's business cannot wait," said Hardwicke with a smile.

"Nor can hairdressers," rejoined Lady Crosby, "and mine will be here in half-an-hour."

Mr Anson, recognising his cue, made his adieux, receiving the farewells of the ladies in return. A firm handclasp from Hardwicke, sword and hat from the obsequious footman, and he was ushered out into the dusty sunshine of Downing Street.

A distant rumble of thunder in the south augured none so well for his journey tomorrow but Anson heard it with half an ear. Elizabeth Yorke's last glance, a long one as

30

she sank in a curtsey at parting, lingered in his mind. His experience told him he was not mistaken; Elizabeth had conceived a kindness for him. He was more amused than surprised, for it was twenty years since he had first discovered that women were attracted to him, but he had scarcely thought of her as a woman. A queer girl altogether, he reflected as he turned left into Whitehall. Nothing but a farrago of nonsense about ships and men while he and she were tête-à-tête and then that revealing glance a moment before he departed. Well, it would be two years, perhaps three, before they met again and there were more urgent matters to be considered. What, for instance, would Norris do with those five hundred soldiers supposed even now to be approaching Portsmouth?

The sooner he was back on board *Centurion* the better.

3

The good fortune of which Anson had boasted to the Lord Chancellor did not hold for his ride to Portsmouth. Heavy rains during the night had turned the roads into sloughs through which the sorry hacks he bestrode, furnished by the posting-stations, made lamentably slow progress. His sole comfort was that he had chosen to ride rather than travel by the lumbering stage-coach, which would have to be manhandled out of the quagmire by its passengers every few miles. Even so, nightfall and a heavy thunderstorm overtook him three miles short of Petersfield and he put up at the inn there for the night.

It was ten o'clock of a bright morning more suited to the season when he steered a way through the throngs in Portsmouth High Street, a boy behind him carrying his valise and cloak, and came out on the busy quays. From the hill-brow of the road behind the port he had caught a glimpse of *Centurion*'s big brown hull and three masts among the clustered shipping in the harbour, and he had experienced precisely the same emotions as young George Anson had felt thirty years ago, arriving home for the holidays from school. This was a homecoming, and something more. On that high poop-deck, in the great cabin beneath it, he would be in his kingdom; when the courses filled and she headed for a landless horizon he would be in his right element again. In London he was plain Mr Anson with lodgings in Killick Street, but here he was Commodore Anson of the Royal Navy.

Centurion was at moorings—not alongside, which would have encouraged desertion—a cable's-length out from one of the further quays. He walked along the slippery paving with noise and bustle and colour on every hand. Men rolling barrels or staggering under heavy spars, men yo-hoing as they hauled bales of stores up to warehouse doors, women in tawdry finery crying their stock of sugared buns or fresh strawberries; shirts red and blue and yellow, tarry breeches and pink-striped cotton trousers. A denser mass of colour caught Anson's eye as he approached the quay opposite *Centurion*. Scarlet above and blue below, it recalled a series of somewhat puzzling encounters when he had left Petersfield; straggling groups of men journeying northward on foot, all of them clad in dark-blue breeches and scarlet coats. Many of them had been limping heavily, some swinging themselves along on crutches. He had thought them wounded soldiers lately disembarked after some military venture, until he had seen that they were all old men. He came nearer, and saw that the blue-and-red mass was a crowd of men clothed like those he had seen on the road. Amid an uproar of shouting and counter-shouting they were being embarked in boats at the direction of a young man whom Anson recognised as Peircy Brett, second lieutenant of the *Gloucester*.

With horrid suspicion dawning in his mind, Anson quickened his pace. He was near enough now to see one of the redcoats, a shrunken veteran with long white hair, borne out of the crowd and deposited on a pile of sacks, collapsed and immobile. Brett, with a despairing gesture, ordered two of his comrades to tend him and then turned to find himself facing the Commodore. He was Anson's junior by thirteen years and looked younger. His square fresh-coloured face wore an expression between pity and anger.

"What's this, Mr Brett?" Anson demanded evenly, touching his hat as the lieutenant doffed his in salute.

"The—troops, sir, from London." Brett's wide grey eyes held a hint of accusation. "Thirteen wagon-loads arrived yesterday. There's supposed to be five hundred but a lot of 'em deserted before we could stop it—as many as had strength to walk, I'd say. I've numbered the rest as they embarked and there's no more than two hundred and sixty. Sir, you never saw such a—"

"Of what regiment?"

"The Invalid Regiment, sir. That's what it's called on the draft-note. They're Chelsea pensioners, in fact." Brett's emotions got the better of him. "It's—it's tragic, sir. These poor old fellows—half of them are over sixty and the rest cripples. It's a sin and a shame to put them aboard ship, let alone expect them to storm a Spanish fort. I don't know who ordered it but I'd like to—"

"That will do, Mr Brett," said Anson curtly. "Where's your captain?"

Brett tried to make his ingenuous countenance as devoid of expression as the Commodore's. "Captain Norris is on board *Gloucester*, sir. He has a vomiting fever and can't leave his cot. Mr Saunders is with him, sir, consulting about what to do with these—troops, sir."

Saunders was *Centurion*'s first lieutenant, an able and conscientious officer but lacking in the sort of initiative that was needed now. But what could be done? Behind his outward calm Anson's mind was furiously at work. Too late now to make any attempt to get these pensioners and cripples exchanged for useful soldiers yet some sort of land-fighting force he must have.

"By'r leave, sir," Brett said hastily, turning. "Bos'n! This

33

last boatload goes to *Severn*. Report to Captain Legge."

Anson's eye fell on a lame redcoat, with one withered calf half the thickness of its fellow, being helped into the boat by two brawny seamen. Hardwicke could not be aware that he was being supplied with such material; Newcastle, from what he had heard of the Duke, would neither know nor care. Well, he would play the cards he'd been dealt, as always, and Fortune and George Anson between them should turn the trick—for one of the cards in his hand was the new Port Admiral, Sir John Balchen, a sound Tory well-disposed towards the Expedition. An interview with the Admiral required better clothes than his mud-spattered riding gear. He would go on board *Centurion* and change. He turned to Brett and found him engaged with an elderly man in red and blue whose left eye-socket was empty under its closed lid.

"Well, what is it?" Brett was demanding.

"It's old Charlie," quavered the man. "Old Charlie Binns—'e's dead."

He jerked a thumb at the pile of sacks. Brett drew in his breath sharply, caught Anson's cold eye upon him, and recovered himself.

"Very well," he said quickly. "I'll see to him. Now get aboard that boat. Tally's two hundred and fifty-nine now, sir," he added to the Commodore.

Anson retrieved his cloak and valise from the boy, who had strayed to look at the dead man, and tossed the lad a coin. "Get me a boat for *Centurion* at once, Mr Brett, if you please. Then see the port authorities about the disposal of the body."

"Aye, sir," Brett said stiffly with a hand to his hat.

As he hurried to obey he thought to himself, not for the first time, that the Commodore had ice in his veins instead of blood.

Since there was no naval boat available at the quays it was a harbour wherry that took the Commodore across to his ship. He eyed her with affection as they approached; the brown hull with its high poop and curling beak-head, the thirteen gunports of the lower deck (they were almost on the waterline, so heavily was she burdened with stores) and the towering masts with their yards crossed ready for sailing. His ship. His home. He could see a bustle of preparation on deck at the entry port; Saumarez, his first lieutenant, would be in charge and Saumarez had espied him. A discordant shrilling of boatswains' pipes greeted him as he clambered up the steep tumblehome of *Centurion*'s side and a double rank of marines presented muskets when he stepped over the rail. At the inboard end of the rank Saumarez awaited him hat in hand, tall and lean and with his own black hair tied in a neat queue as usual. His harsh features showed genuine relief at his captain's return.

Anson glanced quickly about him as he walked forward, noting the hands at work at various shipboard tasks along the upper deck and a party rigging the spritsail yard under the direction of a petty officer. Beyond the long bowsprit he could see *Gloucester* at her moorings and beyond her again *Severn*, with a boatload of red-and-blue Invalids alongside.

"Welcome aboard, sir." Saumarez had noticed the direction of his glance. "*Centurion*'s—ah—military are all below, sir. Ninety's our quota. I've found quarters for seventy-seven for'ard abaft the cable tier but I've had to put thirteen in the hospital for the surgeon to look after. Two of 'em have got the ague, sir."

"Thank you, Mr Saumarez," said Anson without expression.

"Sir!" exploded the first lieutenant. "It's infamous—it's an insult, by God! To saddle us with a parcel of granddads, and not a man but's maimed or palsied! And the quotas for the other ships are no better. Devil take me if I've ever—"

"Thank you, Mr Saumarez!" Anson said again, more loudly. "I'm aware of their condition. Have my gig manned and alongside in half-an-hour, if you please. And pass the word for my steward."

"Aye, sir." Saumarez swallowed his wrath. "Bussey's already come aft, I believe."

Richard Walter, *Centurion*'s chaplain, was waiting to greet the Commodore, his pale studious face contorted in a toothy smile. Anson spared him a nod and went quickly into the great cabin under the poop. Bussey, his wizen-faced steward, had flung a cloth over the round table and was placing wine and a platter of biscuits on it. He dismissed Bussey and heard, as the man went out, the clatter and stamp of a marine sentry taking post outside the cabin door. Now he had the privacy he valued and needed. The equanimity it was his habit and pride to display in every crisis had come near to being ruffled back there on the quay.

He poured himself a glass of madeira and drank it off before getting a pair of white breeches and a coat of claret-coloured satin from the locker on the bulkhead. The forenoon sunlight was striking in through the quarter-lights whose leaning glass panels overlooked the glitter of the harbour waters. He stood by the windows to change his clothes, alternating the buckling and buttoning with a sip of wine or a nibble of biscuit. On this beam the other vessels of his squadron were all in sight, *Pearl* and *Wager* and the diminutive sloop *Tryal*. Their yards, like *Centurion*'s, were crossed ready to sail; and sail they should, he told himself with a frown—in four days' time, whether the Port Admiral could find him any able-bodied troops or not.

He fastened his neckcloth and poured himself another glass of wine. He knew that several hundred marines were quartered in or near Portsmouth undergoing training and he intended to persuade Sir John Balchen, by every means in his power, to transfer some of them to the Expedition. Four days gave far too little time for the exchanging of dispatches with London in an attempt to get rid of his Invalids; and in any case he was not going to invite the almost inevitable rebuff. Just possibly the sending of these incompetents was the result of malice on the part of some Whig politician but he did not think so; it was more likely that they were literally the only troops that the Army, currently reduced and ill-prepared for a war, could spare. So he would sail with them. They were next to useless, merely extra mouths to consume the stores that filled every available space in all six vessels, but it was odds that half of them would be dead before the squadron reached the South Sea. George Anson and his attendant Fortune would see to it that they did not interfere with the success of the Expedition.

He opened his mouth to shout for Ham, remembered that his servant would not reach Portsmouth until tomorrow at earliest, and took a dress sword and his best hat from the locker. He did not really doubt that he would win what he wanted from Balchen, but he was not going to neglect anything that might prepossess the Admiral in his favour.

4

Admiral Balchen found 210 marines and Lieutenant-Colonel Mordaunt Cracherode to supplement Commodore Anson's Expedition. The fact that all the men were new recruits who had never fired a musket did not alter Anson's conviction that Fortune stood ever at his side. But in the twelve weeks that followed there were moments when—though his faith in himself never faltered—he almost believed that his ally had deserted him.

With Balchen's reinforcements distributed on board *Centurion, Gloucester,* and *Severn*, he kept his resolve and sailed from Portsmouth harbour on June 30th. He got as far as the Spit Buoy before a fast Admiralty cutter overtook him with new orders. He was to anchor off St Helens and await the collection of a large convoy which his ships were to escort. Anson had of course to obey. His six ships, and with them the small store-ships *Anna* and *Industry* which were to replenish his supplies before he entered the Pacific, waited day after day while the convoy gathered in driblets from a dozen different ports, 124 merchantmen and 21 small warships bound for destinations as diverse as Turkey, the Indies, and America. During these weeks of tossing at anchor nineteen men of the Invalid Regiment died and were "buried" overside.

Four of Anson's captains conferred with him on board *Centurion*. Norris of the *Gloucester*, the one absentee, was too ill to attend. Legge of the *Severn*, Mitchell of the *Pearl*, Murray of the *Tryal* and Dandy Kidd of the *Wager* were all men stout of heart and tried seamen; as seamen they fulminated at this crass stupidity of Admiralty that set their departure farther and farther from the favourable season for their voyage. Hitherto his captains had imitated Anson's own stoicism in the face of frustration but now they laid the irremediable defects frankly before him: the inefficiency of their crews, the dubious seaworthiness of *Gloucester* and *Wager*, the thousand-and-one shortcomings that demonstrated that neither Admiralty nor Government had the least enthusiasm for the Pacific venture. Dandy Kidd, fiery and plain-speaking, put into words what they were hinting.

"It's not by your fault, sir, that this Expedition's doomed to failure," he said gruffly. "You've kicked against the pricks long enough. To my mind you've got no course but to resign your command."

Anson had heard them out in silence, his beak-nosed face devoid of all expression. He replied evenly, incisively, his pale-blue eyes upon them like the glint of ice.

"To my mind I have no course but obey my orders. You will obey mine. That is all, gentlemen."

He sat working in his cabin that night and far into the morning watch, with Richard Walter writing at his dictation. Next day all the ships of the squadron received detailed orders amplifying those he had already issued regarding gun-drills and seamanship training, and from then on the anchorage was daily loud with rumble of gun-trucks and the yells of petty officers while reluctant processions of pressed men and one-time gaolbirds clawed and clung their way up and down shrouds and out on to yardarms. The few that actively resented the relentless hounding of the bosun's mates, raising an angry fist or giving a back-answer, received the flogging they had been told to expect in such a case. Spreadeagled on a grating,with the whole ship's company paraded to mark and learn the penalty of not instantly obeying an order, they were given a dozen with the cat-o'-nine-tails; Anson never ordered more for offences of this nature. As required by King's Regulations, the captain and all officers not engaged on urgent duty were present on these occasions. The first lieutenant, watching the Commodore's stern immobility from the corner of his eye, could discern no trace of any sort of feeling on those set features. Saunders hated flogging with an intensity rare in a lieutenant of a King's ship; though he was well aware that fear of pain and death was the one sure way of making these sweepings of the prisons and brothels into a crew. Anson was at least not one of those captains (and Saunders knew of more than one) who delighted in the sight of torn flesh and human agony. But neither would he allow sentiment to interfere with the conversion of his ship's company from a herd of fumbling incompetents into fighting seamen.

That conversion was slowly taking place, but the drills and practices continued unabated. And seamanship was not the only skill receiving attention. Daily *Centurion*'s upper deck resounded to the ragged tramp of successive detachments of marines and Invalids at drill under Cracherode's raw subalterns, with little Colonel Cracherode himself damning his guts and liver unceasingly at their incompetence.

And so the summer days passed on towards autumn while the huge convoy gathered, until on September 20th the tale of ships was complete. At last the Commodore's broad pendant soared up to *Centurion*'s masthead and the signal to make sail fluttered from her yardarm; at long last the Expedition began to move down Channel, in company with the concourse of merchantmen. They had waited twelve weeks to perform a convoy duty lasting five days. On the 25th Anson's six ships, with the two store-ships, set a course for Madeira, their first port-of-call on the long voyage to the Pacific.

> *After a passage of 40 days I arrived here with the Squadron of H.M. Ships under my command, during which time we buried two of the Invalid captains. I have given leave to Captain Norris* (Gloucester) *to return to England for the recovery of his health. The ships being all watered I intend to proceed tomorrow to sea.*
>
> G. ANSON

So wrote the Commodore from Madeira on November 2nd. He could hardly have said less. Among other things omitted from this dispatch to the Duke of Newcastle was the fact that unprecedented storms and head-winds had caused a passage that normally took twelve days to extend into a forty-day struggle with high seas, whose continuous battering had ended the miserable existence of another seventeen Invalid soldiers as well as of the two captains he mentioned. Also unmentioned was some news, received from the Portuguese governor of Madeira, which went far to restore Anson's confidence in his ally Fortune.

Portugal was neutral in the present war between England and Spain. But the governor, like most of his countrymen, was more friendly disposed towards the English than towards the Spaniards and did not scruple to tell Anson all that he could. A squadron of eight Spanish warships had been cruising off Madeira for some weeks, their topsails sighted daily by the governor's lookouts until two days ago when they had disappeared beyond the horizon. A Portuguese vessel had been stopped and her master questioned by the Spanish admiral, Don José Pizarro, who had expressed incredulity that no English squadron had yet reached the port of Funchal; the master

(who understood Spanish) had learned from the comments interchanged by Don José and his officers that they
had definite information that such a squadron was to
leave England on the last day of June, and that they had
sailed to intercept it west of Madeira. He had noted that
the guns carried by the Spanish ships, five of which were
first-rates, numbered at least 300.

Anson heard all this on the day of his arrival at
Funchal, where he had to spend a week repairing the
damage done by the storms and filling his water-casks.
There was no sighting of the Spanish squadron during
the week and it was safe to assume that the ships had
given him up and returned to base. And now he could
perceive how narrowly he had escaped disaster. Against a
Spanish fleet of such force his own ships with their
half-trained crews must have been sunk or captured or at
best left so crippled that they could not go on with the
Expedition. In the frustrations and delays in the Channel,
the adverse gales on the Madeira passage, he now saw the
kindly hand of Fortune outstretched to save her favourite.
Had Fortune abated only two days of those delays he
would have been lost.

No thought of Kitty Clive entered his head at this time.
And if anyone had sought to hint that Kitty's hand, rather
than Fortune's, had brought about the circumstance by
which the Spaniards had missed him he would have
laughed and dismissed the idea as absurd. To George
Anson human beings were no more than tools to assist
him in his purpose. They could not influence the destiny
which he believed—now more firmly than ever—he held
in his own two hands.

There were changes in command before the Expedition
could proceed. Norris, a very sick man, had been sent
back to England in a merchant vessel and Mitchell took
his place as captain of *Gloucester*, Dandy Kidd transferring
to *Pearl*. Murray now commanded *Wager* and Lieutenant
Cheap was promoted to command the sloop *Tryal*. Thus
reorganised, the squadron sailed from Madeira on

41

November 3rd, southward bound to "annoy and distress the Spaniards" on the other side of the world. All on board expected to be about that business early in the New Year of 1741.

TWO

Unknown to Fame

1

Centurion was surging along with a bone in her teeth under all plain sail, her progress transmuting the dark-blue rollers of the South Atlantic into dazzling fountains of spray that flew at regular intervals across her thrusting beakhead. The noonday sun, almost overhead, made rainbows at her bow and set the gilding all a-glitter on the elaborate carving that surrounded her stern-galleries. She was like a creature set free and joyous; free of the sou'-westers that had for so long forced her to tack, and tack, and tack again until at last the South-East Trades had made their benevolent presence felt. Now she was able to hold a steady course for the squadron's rendez-vous off the Brazil coast, the island of Santa Catarina.

On this day, the second of December, all Commodore Anson's ships were sailing in company. Two miles away to leeward *Gloucester* and *Severn*, with *Pearl* and *Wager* beyond them, sped on their parallel course like low-flying seagulls. Since leaving Madeira a month ago the sloop *Tryal* had been ordered to sail in advance of the rest so as to give early notice of any Spanish vessels that might be sighted; Anson was taking no chance of running un-awares into Pizarro's squadron. With *Tryal* was the little store-ship *Anna*, and the two ships, or rather their upper sails, could be discerned as white specks on the bar of the horizon ahead. The other store-ship, *Industry*, had turned homeward a fortnight ago as she was entitled to do by the terms of her charter, but Gerrard of the *Anna* had boldly announced his wish to stay with the Expedition to the end—a wish which Anson was only too happy to grant, for all his fighting-ships were already so crammed with stores that their crews would have been seriously hampered in a sea-fight if more were added. So there were seven ships running southward with a fair wind, a wind that mercifully abated the heat of the equatorial sun to the greater comfort of the two thousand men in them.

The Commodore in *Centurion*'s stern cabin felt the heat smiting down through the poop-deck overhead and sat back from the chart he was studying to pass a kerchief over his damp brow. At a little desk under the larboard window Richard Walter the chaplain was scribbling industriously in a manuscript book, his cadaverous face creased in concentration as he penned the official record of the voyage. Ham, Anson's Negro servant, squatted in a dark corner playing with a kitten that had come on board at Funchal. Bright discs of light, reflections from *Centurion*'s bubbling wake, winked and slid across the deckhead above. Anson's glance took in his immediate surroundings, his ears gathered the familiar sounds of his ship's progress through a moderate sea with a beam wind, and those two senses brought him satisfaction that would have been complete but for the intervention of a third sense. Intermittently there came to his nostrils, on the wayward draughts that entered the cabin, a faint but penetrating smell, a stink of putrescence impossible to ignore.

Anson frowned. He would never have admitted it, but the intrusive stink appeared to him a sort of *lèse-majesté*. The cabin of a captain of a King's ship was his sanctum and watch-tower, whose position right aft in the high poop symbolised his lofty separation from the half-thousand lesser men who crowded the lower deck and were subject to the first lieutenant and his underlings. From this inviolable privacy the captain might come forth on occasion, and from it he would direct the actions of his subordinates, over whom he held the power of life and death. This remoteness, as of a god, was traditional in the Royal Navy since before the Dutch Wars and Anson considered it essential to the maintenance of his command. It was a small but disturbing circumstance that a stink from the lower deck should penetrate to the very throne-room.

With a shrug of the shoulders he dismissed the matter from his thoughts and returned to the chart. Ten minutes ago the master had reported the result of the noon sights and the distance run by dead-reckoning and he had marked the squadron's position. The latitude would be accurate enough but longitude, with chronometers so liable to err, was less easy to determine. If they had in fact crossed the Line in 27° West Longitude all was well, but the reports of mariners suggested that there was a strong south equatorial current setting west, setting a ship as much as thirty miles westward from her course each day. To allow for that—

His calculations were interrupted by the clashing salute of the sentry and a knock on the cabin door, heralding the entrance of the first lieutenant. Charles Saunders's mild and somewhat melancholy countenance was grave.

"Your pardon, sir," he said to Anson; and to the chaplain, "We're ready for you now, Mr Walter."

Walter took a black-bound book from a drawer in the desk and rose to his feet, ducking a bow at the Commodore and giving him a look that was half apology and half inquiry. Anson shook his head.

"Is Mr Saumarez on deck?" he asked Saunders.

"Yes, sir."

"My compliments to Mr Saumarez, Mr Walter, and he will please to take charge."

The chaplain went out, leaving the first lieutenant standing hat in hand and plainly with something to say. Anson spoke first.

"How many?" he demanded abruptly.

"Three, sir."

"Seamen?"

"One seaman, sir, and two soldiers—Invalid regiment." Saunders hesitated. "That makes eighteen since we left Madeira, and the other ships will have had losses in proportion, likely as not. There are bound to be—"

"I know it." The Commodore cut him short. "Every other day since Madeira I've made one at a funeral party on the upper deck. To be plain with you, I consider these funerals are Walter's business rather than mine. From now on he'll read the service and the officer of the watch will supervise."

He got up and stood at the window overlooking the upper deck, his hands linked behind his back. He could see Walter, the prayer-book open in his hands and the breeze fluttering the black gown he always wore, between the two ranks of marines at the lee rail, and the three planks with their ends resting on the rail each with a canvas-swathed figure stretched motionless upon it.

"We've sixty-nine sick, can't move from their hammocks," said Saunders. "There's as many more barely able to tail on to a rope—and then only for fear of the bosun's rattan."

"With scurvy that's to be expected," said Anson without looking round.

Saunders bit his lip, his eye on the Commodore's broad back, and after a moment braced himself to speak.

"It's also to be expected that a great many more will die, sir, if conditions below decks stay as they are. There's the Invalids—only a few of them can be used for ship duties and the rest are weak or old or seasick so they stay in their hammocks. That's besides the sixty-nine sick men and the watch below, sir. It means fifteen inches a man for hammock-space. They're so packed that Ettrick the surgeon can't shove his head up between 'em, let alone use his blood-letting gear. And the air down there's not fit for a hog to breathe. The stink's worse than a midden— you get a whiff of it even here, I notice. And we're so heavy laden, sir, so low in the water, that the lower-deck

46

gunports can't be opened to give ventilation." He repressed a shudder. "I was down below half-an-hour ago and I—well, it'd shock any humane person, sir."

Anson had heard him out without shifting his position. Below him on the upper deck he saw the chaplain raise his hand and heard Saumarez's harsh voice give a command. One after another the planks were tilted and the three bodies in their canvas lashings launched into the depths overside. The ranks of marines turned smartly inboard and marched away for'ard, the gilt on their pointed shakos twinkling in the blithe sunshine. He turned and went to sit at the table.

"Please to sit down, Mr Saunders."

He indicated the chair opposite him, which like his own chair and the table was bolted to the deck. After a momentary hesitation the first lieutenant seated himself.

"You seem to imply, Mr Saunders, that I am not a humane person," said Anson without rancour.

"By no means, sir!" the lieutenant said hastily. "I meant that I myself was shocked. The conditions—"

"Ah, yes. It's not escaped my notice that you have a certain—um—softness, unusual in an officer. Well, I have a laden ship and scurvy aboard. You know as well as I do that a vessel on a voyage such as ours is fortunate indeed if she escapes scurvy. No one knows what causes scurvy and there's no cure for it. *Centurion*'s complement is four hundred men and we have to carry more than twice that number for the purpose of this Expedition, so accommodation below decks is cramped. Since you've exerted yourself to bring to my notice what I'm already well aware of, I presume you have some remedy to suggest."

The Commodore, his hard blue stare on his first lieutenant, had to wait for Saunders's halting answer.

"I—er—I'm certain, sir, that lack of fresh air is aggravating the sickness. Mr Ettrick is of the same opinion, sir. If it was possible for some ventilation to be arranged—"

"Jettison half my stores so that the lower-deck ports can

47

be opened?" Anson cut in. "You know that's impossible. The stores are vital to my success." He leaned back in his chair, and his voice, though equable still, took on a harder tone. "Mark this, Mr Saunders. His gracious Majesty and their lordships of the Admiralty have ordained this Expedition, the ships to carry it out, the men to be borne in them. My charge is to do my duty with the means I've been given, be the ships or the men sound or rotten, and I shall do it. Neither foul winds nor scurvy shall hinder me, though I can no more prevent their annoyance than I can add extra accommodation in *Centurion*'s 'tween-decks. I trust I don't need to add that your whole duty is to obey my orders?"

"Of course not, sir," Saunders said quickly.

"Then that is all," said Anson.

The first lieutenant was at the cabin door when the Commodore's voice halted him.

"Oh, Mr Saunders—see to it that the surgeon and his mates are diligent in their tasks. And double the working-parties detailed to swab out the sick quarters."

"Aye, sir."

There was little alleviation for Saunders's wounded self-esteem in those orders. He was thinking, as he went down to the upper deck, of something he had overheard six months ago in the George Inn at Portsmouth. "Anson?" one naval captain had said to another. "He's oak and iron, not flesh and blood."

In the cabin Anson was frowning at the chart without seeing its spidery lines and crosses. Aware of something tapping at his shoe-buckle, he bent and picked up the kitten, fondling it absently for a moment before handing it to Ham, who had jumped up to rescue his playmate.

"Stow her out of harm's way," he told the Negro. "And Ham—bring your flute and give me some music."

While his servant was gone he took from a bulkhead rack a roll of stiff paper and laid it out on the table. It was the shipbuilder's drawing of *Centurion* stripped of her planking to reveal her structural beams and timbers. He was considering this intently when Ham returned and began to play very softly and sweetly on his flute. The melody he chose was the Minuet from *Berenice*, and the familiar notes drew the Commodore from his studies to a world now far away in space and time. Vauxhall Gardens, Kitty Clive singing to Mr Handel's harpsichord accompaniment, the lodging in Killick Street, Lord Hardwicke's study—a different world indeed from this. And a different man, that undistinguished gentleman who had played courtier to the Lord Chancellor and bandied inanities over tea with Lady Crosby. Also, of course, there had been Elizabeth Yorke with her quaint eagerness. Odd that some words of hers should sound in his mind now, about ships being but wooden shells—*whether they can beat the Spaniards depends on the men in them*. He was thinking something of the sort now, though not on the same lines as his first lieutenant. Saunders's anxieties were for men as mere human beings. He, Anson, thought of them as topmen and gunners and reefers, seamen or fighting-men in some station essential to the fulfilment of his mission. It was just conceivable, as he had now allowed himself to admit, that scurvy might take so many of his men that not enough would be left to fill those vital stations.

He pored long over the drawing of *Centurion*'s oaken ribs and spine. And next day, the wind falling away and making contact between ships possible, the squadron received orders which were already being carried out in *Centurion*:

> *To the Captains of all Ships: For the better controlling of the Scurvy, you will immediately have six air scuttles cut for ventilation, in places where they will least weaken the structure of the ship.*

It was done. But foul air, it seemed, was not after all a factor in the aggravation of scurvy. In the ensuing fortnight the disease spread with startling swiftness in all seven ships with its horrible concomitants of fever, rotting bones and flesh, vomiting and bodily weakness. Men took

to their hammocks and died within hours; or simply fell
dead as they crossed the deck. Two days of gales doubled
the death-rate. The weather improved again, and having
sighted the Brazil coast on December 16th the squadron
anchored on the 20th in a wide bay of the Portuguese
island of Santa Catarina, each vessel a floating makeshift
hospital burdened with sick and dying men.

2

"If Saint Catherine had spent three weeks on this
island," said Peircy Brett, flinging sweat from his crimson
brow, "she'd have found it a pleasant relief to be broken
on the wheel."

"That was Catherine of Alexandria, Mr Brett,"
returned Walter the chaplain gravely. "The Spaniards
would name this place after Catherine of Siena."

"Well, whichever it was the Dons were fools," Brett said
wearily. "No saint would have anything to do with an
island that's as hot as hell in January."

He cast himself down on the parched grass in the shade
of the broad-leaved tree which the chaplain was using as a
shelter against the fierce heat of the sun, and stared out
across the brown foreshore at his ship, *Gloucester*, lying
two cable-lengths from the beach with five other ships
anchored in line with her. The seventh ship, *Tryal*, was
careened on the shingle a quarter of a mile away, where
she had been hove-up with immense toil after all her guns
and stores had been taken out of her.

At this point on the arc of the bay a wide clearing
stretched for half-a-mile along the coast and made an
indentation in the wall of dark-green forest that rose in
tree-clad hills farther inland. The clearing, sparsely
dotted with trees and devoid of roads or buildings, was a
long cannon-shot from the few houses of the Portuguese
settlement which could be seen on a slight rise on the
coast to northward. It had become suddenly populous

three weeks ago when Anson had caused fourteen large tents to be erected, using sailcloth and spare yards, and brought ashore the sick men of the squadron, numbering more than three hundred. Hot though it was on shore, there was more light and air to be had in an open-ended tent than in the stinking darkness of a ship's 'tween-decks; but the hope that the disease would be arrested had been frustrated. A few, the strongest, had indeed recovered. Eighty-four had died. Yet in each of the fourteen tents there were still at least twenty sick and every day men were dying, while Ettrick and his weary assistants toiled in vain. Peircy Brett had served twelve years in the Navy but had never been in action. Death he had seen but never on such a scale as this, and at first he had been sickened and saddened by the lavish waste of lives. He had lately become more hardened, for he had been put in charge of the grave-digging. He and the chaplain had naturally been thrown much together and this shade-tree was their customary post of observation; from it all the hospital tents could be seen, as well as the graveyard some distance behind them where teams of men were even now at work with spade and mattock.

"I must go," said Walter suddenly.

A figure had appeared outside one of the tents and raised an arm. The chaplain stalked away towards the tent, his inordinately lean shanks moving fast despite the heat; a man was at the point of death and needed the spiritual comfort it was his duty to give if he could get there in time. Brett hoisted himself to his feet—the effort made the sweat trickle inside his already soaked clothing—and scanned the graveyard, shading his eyes against the glare. Three heaps of newly-turned black earth. That should suffice for a while and the poor devils he could see snatching a rest in the meagre shade of a bush could take their ease. He sat down again in his own patch of shade, luxuriating in one of the intervals of leisure his present job allowed him. The job that preceded it had been the most arduous he could remember.

51

The Commodore had ordered every ship to be emptied of stores and gear and men's personal belongings, and that had taken five days of continuous hard work. Then he had had all holds and cabins smoked, with bundles of smouldering rags and rubbish amalgamated with moss collected from the forest. Then the ships' interiors from upper decks to bilges had been scrubbed with vinegar and finally swabbed out. Peircy Brett, supervising and inspecting below decks on board *Gloucester,* had thought he would never get out of his nostrils the abominable stink of the filth that had gone overboard. And then all the gear and stores had to be taken back on board and stowed. In the middle of this activity it had been discovered that *Tryal's* mainmast was sprung and her foremast so rotten that the next hard blow would bring it down by the board. Four days of searching in the forest had proved that Brazilian forests did not provide the sort of trees from which masts could be made, and application to the Portuguese governor had met with a flat refusal to supply replacement spars. So both *Tryal's* masts had to be fished, by lashing strong timbers round the weak places; a feeble expedient, Brett knew, for the facing of the gales they were sure to encounter round the Horn.

A movement near the tents caught his eye. Two men carrying a stretcher had emerged and were taking another corpse towards the burial-ground. Walter walked after them with hands clasped behind back holding his prayer-book. Some distance away a score of men of the off-duty watch were gathered, stark naked, round a blazing fire—the combined heat of fire and sun must be almost unbearable. They were using smouldering twigs in an attempt to rid their clothes of lice, rubbing the red-hot ends along the seams. The sight made Brett wriggle and scratch. He was by no means free from vermin himself; they were an inevitable curse of life on shipboard. But it wouldn't do for an officer to strip and join the men over there. He wondered whether the Commodore suffered similarly.

52

By turning his head to look along the coast to northward he could see Anson's tent, an open-ended shelter like the others, beyond a clump of feathery trees. There was a conference taking place in there now; Captains Mitchell, Legge and Murray, and Cheap of the *Tryal*, but not Kidd who was laid low with scurvy. He could picture Anson presiding, rigidly upright, beak-nosed and hard-eyed, to all appearance totally unaffected by the devastating heat, receiving reports and issuing his orders as though he was comfortably at anchor in Spithead. Brett had a great affection for his own captain; Mathew Mitchell was a first-rate seaman of the hearty hard-swearing kind, loud in praise or blame and as human in his vices, which included over-fondness of the bottle, as he was in his virtues of geniality and courage. For Anson, Brett could feel no affection though he admired him enormously. The Commodore, he felt, was almost superhuman in his detachment from the fears and anxieties that occupied the minds of his subordinates, yet every detail of their present difficult situation was being dealt with by him with an efficiency that showed that nothing escaped him. It must have been a severe disappointment to him, when he reached Santa Catarina with his ships in such a terrible condition, to find that the governor of the little Portuguese settlement was hand-in-glove with the Spaniards and would afford him no assistance. But he had merely gone straight ahead with the work that had to be done as though he had expected nothing else. Brett told himself that this cold devotion to purpose was exactly what was needed in an Expedition leader. And yet in any venture demanding his utmost courage and loyalty he would rather have followed Mathew Mitchell.

The four captains were coming out of the Commodore's tent now, to walk slowly across to the beach where their boats waited. The Commodore himself emerged; he stood a moment to scan the ships lying at anchor and then clapped his three-cornered hat on his head and began to walk towards Brett's shade-tree. The lieutenant hastily got to his feet and brushed a throng of intrusive ants from his breeches. Anson was as always neatly dressed, his white stockings spotless and the silver buckles of his shoes winking in the sunlight. Brett, conscious of a tarry stain on the knee of his breeches and a ragged tear in his coat, adjusted his loosened neckcloth and lifted his hat as the Commodore approached.

"Good afternoon, Mr Brett," Anson said, stopping. "Another burial, I see."

"Yes, sir," said Brett. "The fifth today."

"And the total so far?"

"This makes eighty-five, sir, including *Tryal*'s gunner and two master's mates from *Gloucester*. Most of them, though, were Invalid Regiment men."

"Yes," said Anson absently; he seemed to be making mental calculations.

"There's a lot more won't last the week, sir," Brett went on. It was unreasoning to feel resentment rising in him. It wasn't Anson's fault that this was happening.

"It's—it's a terrible thing to see them dying in such numbers," he burst out, "every ship's company dwindling day by day like this. Isn't there anything—anything more—we can do to stop it, sir?"

For a moment something like annoyance showed itself in the Commodore's pale-blue eyes; but his voice as he replied was level and expressionless as ever.

"If there had been, Mr Brett, I would have done it. And you may set your anxieties at rest. When we sail, which will be within the week, there will be ample numbers of men left to work my ships round Cape Horn." His glance went beyond the lieutenant to the burial-ground. "There's a working-party idling. See to it, Mr Brett, if you please."

"Aye, sir."

The Commodore turned away, touching his hat in acknowledgement of Brett's hurried salute. The lieutenant watched him walking, briskly despite the bludgeoning heat, in the direction of the beach where *Tryal* was careened. He was thinking, as he began to move towards the burial-ground and the selection of a spot for the next grave to be dug, that Anson resembled the Automaton devised (so Brett had heard) by some ingenious German; he had been wound up and the appropriate levers pushed to set him on an expedition, and he would carry it out without feeling or emotion. But no, that was inept. This was a thinking Automaton, able to devise means of overcoming obstacles when they occurred. A man, then—but a man without a heart.

The working-party saw him approaching and scrambled to its feet, seven skinny brown figures clad in ragged drawers and nothing more. They were seamen from *Wager* in the charge of a leading seaman named Barnes. One of the seven staggered and fell as soon as he stood up, turned feebly on his side, and vomited into the lower branches of the bush.

"Fowler's got it, sir," said Barnes. "Felt it a-comin' on, he did."

"Very well," said Brett, trying to imitate Anson's imperturbability. "Two of you carry him to the end tent larboard side, and look sharp. The rest come with me."

He walked towards the farther side of the graveyard, trying to forget that he had just seen a man marked for death. Two hundred yards away to his left the chaplain was stalking back to the shade-tree, leaving half-a-dozen men shovelling earth into the newly-occupied grave.

"By'r leave, sir," said Barnes from behind him, "any idee how long afore we sail from here?"

"A week," Brett said shortly.

"Thankee, sir," Barnes said with satisfaction. "We got a bit of a gamble on, d'ye see," he added, plainly concerned to explain and excuse his question. "I'm wagerin' on a hundred deaders by the time we sail, sir, an' at the rate we're goin' I reckon a week'll just about—"

"That'll do!" snapped the lieutenant.

He was revolted by the callousness of men who could run a sweepstake on the number of their shipmates who

would die of a horrible disease in a given time. But he wondered whether Barnes's ghoulish calculations were any more to be condemned than Anson's reckoning-up of the survivors who would work his ships round Cape Horn.

"Start a new row here," he said, halting. "Each grave a fathom and a span, depth four feet, a fathom between graves."

As they started to use mattock and spade he stood back from the work, looking across the long lines of mounds between the dark forest and the blue bar of sea. There could be no headstones, no graven record of those who lay here; only, in the ships' books, the usual marking of "D.D."—Discharged Dead. Peircy Brett had brought two or three books of recent publication with him on this voyage and Mr Pope's version of Homer's *Iliad* was one of them. When death began daily to take its toll he had noted glumly that Pope had well described this inexorable antagonist:

> *Pluto, the grisly god, who never spares*
> *Who feels no mercy, and who hears no prayers.*

He was reflecting now that if (as began to seem doubtful) the Expedition achieved success the names of its commander and his captains would have an honoured place in history even if they died in the endeavour and were buried without headstones. For these others who died in Anson's service Mr Pope had another apt line:

> *The rest were vulgar deaths, unknown to fame.*

3

The squadron sailed from Santa Catarina on a Sunday, January 18th, leaving a hundred and one dead men buried on the island; which assured Seaman Barnes of extra rum every day for a week—a tot from each of his five messmates. Before that week had elapsed the ships of the Expedition were in trouble. A violent gale on the third day after sailing was followed by a persistent thick fog; and when this at last cleared *Pearl* was nowhere to be seen and *Tryal's* fished mainmast had gone overboard taking one seaman with it. *Gloucester* took the damaged sloop in tow and they sailed on through somewhat better weather. The Commodore had named their next rendezvous, the last before the passage round the Horn, as St Julian on the coast of Patagonia, and if *Pearl* had weathered the storm she could be expected to join the rest there.

Death still haunted the 'tween-decks as constantly as ever. *Centurion* had landed eighty sick men on Santa Catarina in the hope of bringing them back to health, but she had re-embarked ninety-six before sailing; the other ships were in like case. Once more there was the endless labour of caring for the sick and dying and trying to keep their quarters clean, the all-pervading stench of vomit and excreta, the perfunctory "burials" overside every day. The six vessels that dropped anchor in good harbourage a little south of the cluster of primitive shanties that was St Julian had each its cargo of human misery.

Yet Anson was not ill-satisfied. He had endured, since he had to, the long stay at Santa Catarina in the knowledge that his squadron was liable to be attacked from the sea by the Spaniards in overwhelming strength, at any time in those last two weeks. Unless they had rounded the Horn, Pizarro and his ships must have gone back from Madeira to Buenos Aires, the largest naval base in Spanish America; and he did not doubt that the governor of Santa Catarina had sent off the urgent news of his arrival as soon as he reached the island. He had cleared that danger for the present, though it was more than likely to recur. He had six of his seven ships in a friendly harbour where the *vaqueros* who tended the vast herds of cattle were glad to sell fresh meat. There was no timber at all on the rolling Patagonian grasslands but he could rig a jury mast on the stump of *Tryal's* mainmast

57

using a spar that *Wager* was carrying in reserve, and while that was being done he could prepare every ship to face the voyage round the Horn at a later and stormier season than he had planned for in England. It needed only the safe arrival of *Pearl* to confirm his belief that Fortune was still on the side of George Anson.

And *Pearl* came, reaching St Julian the day after the Commodore's arrival. The storm had scarcely damaged her but she brought bad news. Captain Dandy Kidd was dead of the scurvy and buried; and Salt, the lieutenant who had taken charge, told of his narrow escape from a fleet of five Spanish warships that could only be Pizarro's squadron.

Anson considered this latter news with concern. If Pizarro had followed him beyond 40° south latitude it meant that the Spanish admiral was determined to catch him. But the Spaniards could not know of the rendezvous at St Julian though they knew he was bound for the Pacific Coast, so they might well assume that he had sailed straight for the passage of the Horn and make for the Horn themselves. He hoped they would. The fact that *Pearl*, the worst sailer in his squadron, had escaped Pizarro by outsailing him suggested that the Spaniards' seamanship was not of the high standard demanded by the Horn. It would not do to assume they would take that course, though. If Pizarro decided to look for him along the coast and caught him here, his ships full of sick men and *Tryal* disabled, that would be the end of his Expedition. Nothing that he had resolved to do at St Julian must be skimped, but all must be done in the shortest time possible.

As usual, the Commodore directed every detail of the work that now occupied all the sound men in the squadron. Not only the gales of the Horn, but also the prospect of a sea-fight had to be prepared for. It had been intended that the *Anna* should transfer the remainder of her stores to the warships here, but the crates and barrels of foodstuffs already took up so much space between the guns that it was barely possible to fire them. Once again the bold John Gerrard, master of the *Anna*, agreed to follow the fortunes of the Expedition, and instead of discharging her cargo his little ship (she was a pink, having a stern as sharp as her bows) took on board as much of the stores as she could hold. Every ship was watered to its full capacity, each rope and spar examined and tested. The lower-deck guns were double-secured with quoins nailed under their trucks and extra lashings to counter the heavy rolling that could be expected in the huge seas of 50° south and beyond. *Tryal's* improvised mast was set up and strengthened as far as could be done.

And now, for the first time, Anson felt the full effect of the losses in manpower he had so far sustained. For the hard work that needed to be done so quickly he could call on only half the numbers with which he had sailed from Madeira fifteen weeks ago, and a proportion of those had to be used for hospital duties; there were 200 men, all told, down with scurvy. The unhappy veterans of the Invalid Regiment had been literally decimated by disease and the rigours of the voyage, and those that were left alive were useless. The available hands, seamen and marines, were driven as hard as any slave-gang, the majority indeed working with a will and the remainder from fear of the bosuns' "starters", the two-foot knotted ropes used for stimulating laggards. Fortunately the climate of St Julian was less hampering to manual labour than that of Santa Catarina. Fifteen hundred miles of southing had brought them within a hundred miles of the fiftieth parallel, and both air and sea held already the chill of the Antarctic waves that were hardly more than a week's sailing away.

The Commodore spent much time with his charts. These were few, and dubiously accurate, for the passage he was about to attempt had been made very rarely and never charted in detail. The crossing of the fiftieth parallel, as he was well aware, constituted a daring feat in itself, a braving of unknown seas where winds and currents obeyed no known laws and successful navigation was dependent as much upon luck as on good seamanship. He had read everything about the Horn he could lay hands on before leaving England, including Lord Stanley's translation of Magellan's account and the *Voyages* of Hakluyt, and it was these that had influenced him in choosing St Julian as a port-of-call. For here both Magellan and Drake had stopped to recuperate and brace themselves for the battle with the terrors of the Horn. Here Ferdinand Magellan, the first circumnavigator, had quelled a mutiny; here Francis Drake had held the trial for mutiny of his friend Doughty, on one of the small islands in the harbourage, and Doughty had been executed. Anson was far from insensitive to historical associations. Where these great men had gone he was going. Beyond lay the object of his mission, and future fame, and Spanish gold. Not his defective ships, nor the perils of the Horn, nor the death that was steadily robbing him of men, should prevent the Expedition's success. Bussey the steward, returning from serving Anson's evening meal as usual, confided to Ham that the Commodore was looking "like a man what's been told 'e's going to 'Eaven".

In cool weather, under a clear pale sky, the ship work progressed while a week and a half passed. On shore, where the coastal strip of pampas stretched away inland to dim blue uplands, occasional groups of leather-clad *vaqueros* or grotesquely-painted Indians watched the activity on the anchored ships and chattered and pointed when the daily burial-parties landed with their burdens. For there was no sign that the scurvy was relaxing its hold, and to its victims were added a few others who had been smitten with a mysterious fever. Among the latter was *Centurion*'s first lieutenant. Saunders was too ill to comprehend the news that Anson had promoted him commander of *Tryal*, Murray having taken over *Pearl* in place of the deceased Kidd and Cheap having been transferred to command *Wager*.

At St Julian Peircy Brett had once again been ordered to take charge of grave-digging and burials, presumably, as he told himself wryly, because he was now deemed to be a specialist and expert in that line. From this duty he was summoned aboard *Centurion* to receive new orders from the Commodore.

"Mr Salt has been directed to carry on your recent tasks, Mr Brett," Anson told him. "You are to transfer immediately from *Gloucester* to *Centurion*, as my second lieutenant."

"Aye, sir," said Brett; he might have added "thank you", but he was not certain yet whether to be pleased or dismayed.

"As Mr Saunders is unable at present to take over his new command," Anson went on, "I am sending Mr Saumarez to *Tryal* in temporary command. You will therefore assume the duties of a first lieutenant *pro tempore*." He paused. "I've not consulted your preferences in this, Mr Brett. As I believe you've noticed, the needs of the Expedition come first and last with me. However, you may think the direction of the living preferable to the disposal of the dead."

"Aye, sir."

Brett could not restrain a grin as he spoke, though it was impossible to decide whether there was a twinkle in Anson's eye or not. At any rate, he thought, as he hastened off to get his gear on board, that was the first time he had detected any trace of humour in the Commodore.

On the tenth day of their stay at St Julian *Tryal*'s refit was completed. Next morning the squadron weighed and sailed, heading now somewhat east of south for the Straits Le Maire between the tip of Tierra del Fuego and the island called Los Estodos by the Spaniards and Staten Island by the British, regarded by early navigators as the boundary between Atlantic and Pacific. Staten Island was a mere 480 sea-miles from St Julian, and Anson, confident in Fortune's aid, expected to make the passage of the

20-mile Straits in a week's time. The island of Juan Fernandez, 1,500 miles north from the Horn, had been named as the main rendezvous in the Pacific should the ships fail to forgather at Socorro Island farther south; but all captains had been ordered, in the strictest terms, to sail their vessels in close company from now on. The Commodore was resolved to have his whole fighting-strength ready to give battle if he should encounter Pizarro's fleet.

Just before they sailed Charles Saunders had suffi-ciently recovered from the fever to take command of *Tryal*, so Peircy Brett—rather to his relief—could relinqu-ish his temporary post to *Centurion*'s proper first lieuten-ant. He got on well with Saumarez, liked his new ship, and had established friendly relations with the kitten Charlotte, who was now four months old and given to perilous explorations in the mizzen-shrouds. The wind blew light and fair and the cold bright days were reminiscent of English weather. Despite the crowded "hospitals" below decks and the increasing death-roll, Brett's spirits rose. He was heading as far south as man had ever sailed, and that adventure was only the gateway to adventures yet to come.

4

"Marines! At*ten*—steady, damn and blast ye!" blared Colonel Cracherode. "Atten-SHUN! Dis-MISS!"

The thirty-three marines in their scarlet coats with white-and-gold facings turned smartly right, paused a moment, and trotted for'ard. Their commanding officer scowled after them before strutting aft towards the wardroom. Cracherode was short, skinny, and elderly, with a wrinkled yellow face that would have been much like a monkey's but for the unfashionable grey moustache he wore, and long service in the West Indies had not improved his naturally peevish temper. He considered he had excuse for peevishness on board *Centurion*. His actual rank of lieutenant-colonel was below that of a naval captain so he took his meals in the wardroom; Anson, who disliked him, never invited him on the rare occasions when the squadron captains dined with the Commodore, though as officer commanding troops he participated in all councils. In addition, Cracherode was annoyed at having less than three dozen men under his immediate command on board. At Portsmouth *Centurion* had embarked seventy-nine marines and *Gloucester* fifty, the rest being divided among the other ships; and the meagre squad he had just dismissed was all that was left alive of the flagship's detachment. It was characteristic of the colonel's contempt for all things nautical that he ignored the hail from the masthead that sent everyone else on deck leaping to the rail or into the shrouds.

"La-a-and ho! Fine on th' stabb'd bow!"

It was a bright morning with a moderate breeze and only the slightest of seas running, and Anson, on the poop with his telescope, was soon able to distinguish a row of snow-capped mountains, jagged as the teeth of a saw, breaking the horizon: Tierra del Fuego, the Land of Fire. There were no smoking volcanoes in sight but there could be no doubt that this was that eastward-curling tip of the South American continent that ended in Cape Horn, stretching farthest south of any land-mass on earth towards the Antarctic ice. In a little while he could discern the upper crest of Staten Island rising to southward of the mainland. He closed his glass with a snap and turned to look at the ships of his squadron, sailing in close company as he had ordered. *Tryal, Anna, Wager, Pearl, Severn, Gloucester*—all speeding beside him with a fair wind towards the entrance to the Pacific Ocean. The Expedition was within reach of its objective. Cape Horn itself, of course, had still to be weathered when he had passed the Straits Le Maire, and they would need to make their southing for some days more in order to get round it. But in a matter of weeks now, he would be striking at the

Spaniards in the heart of their American empire.

Up in the bows Midshipman the Honourable Augustus Van Keppel was receiving instruction in current affairs from Corporal Thompson of the marines, a stocky middle-aged man with shaggy grey eyebrows.

"Mean to say you don't know, sir?" Thompson was saying. "You never heard of Captain Jenkins, now?"

"Not I," said the midshipman. "Was he a Navy captain?"

Keppel was a tall dark youth, a younger son of the Earl of Albemarle. When he had joined *Centurion* he had been fifteen years old and over-fat. Now he was sixteen, and the long frieze greatcoat he wore against the cold wind hung loose on a skeletal body. He had survived a bout of scurvy, one of the very few to do so, and was the only midshipman on board fit for duty; of the others, two had died and the third, Carpenter, was very ill. Keppel had joined the little crowd that had hurried to stand at the for'ard rail and gaze at the land they were approaching. He had wondered aloud why they had come to this godforsaken place to fight Spaniards—why, indeed, they had to fight Spaniards anyway. Thompson was about to enlighten him.

"Merchant captain, Jenkins was," explained the corporal. "The Dons in some Spanish port didn't like his face so they cut off one of his ears. Home he comes with his ear in his pocket and takes it to the House of Commons. 'Take a look at this,' he says, and slams it on the table before them all. 'That's what Spaniards done to an Englishman,' he says. 'Now, then, gents, what'll you do to them Spaniards?' And that, sir, is why we're fighting the Spaniards."

"Remarkable," murmured Keppel. "That is, if it's true."

"It's as true as you're standing there," retorted Thompson a trifle huffily. "And look ye, sir—but for Captain Jenkins and his ear you'd never have seen that bugger up there—nor them buggers down there." He pointed to the albatross cruising with motionless wings above the masthead and the dolphins gambolling below the bowsprit-end. "Nor," he added, "them spiky bits with snow on 'em I can see sticking up ahead."

The mountains of Tierra del Fuego were in sight from the foredeck now and the chatter of the watching men grew louder and more excited.

"I'd give them all for a porterhouse steak and a tankard of good ale," said Keppel.

Thompson grinned. "Now you're talking, sir," he said.

"All hands!" came Saumarez's harsh bellow. "Get the t'gallants on her—main, fore, and mizzen! Jump to it! Mr Keppel, your station's aft here by the mizzen and I'll thank you to keep to it."

The hands swarmed aloft with more dash and energy than they had lately shown. But Peircy Brett, watch in hand by the foot of the foremast, noted that the setting of the topgallant sails took more than twice the normal time: there was only half the usual number of men to do it. The other ships of the squadron increased sail also and the gap between Staten Island and the mainland crept steadily nearer across the wrinkled grey-green water. The favouring breeze still held hour by hour and it would be the plainest possible sailing to pass through the Straits. Two days ago a sudden gale had forced the ships to bring-to under reefed mizzen-sails for a whole day; but here, under the very nose of the Cape whose terrible storms were a byword among mariners, they were slipping along as gaily as in the most sheltered of British waters. Maybe the Horn weather was all a legend, the raw hands surmised; maybe, amended the more knowledge-able, the squadron would be let off with a few days' buffeting. No one knew what the Commodore was thinking, aloof and motionless on the poop-deck.

The great grim cliffs of Staten Island grew out of the sea on their larboard hand, immense and desolate as the ruins of some titanic city, revealing a long wall of shattered rock as they came abeam. Anson watched the forbidding wall gliding slowly past on one side and the saw-toothed coast on the other and thought how frail and small his seven vessels had become in this world of giants. Yet ships even smaller, captains without his navigational advantages, had passed this way. Such sparse information as he possessed concerning the part of the passage beyond the Straits was wholly discouraging, and March 7th (according to that information) was in the middle of the worst season for attempting it; but even he could not help inferring from so auspicious a beginning a triumphant end.

The rock wall of the island ended in a cape of huge tumbled blocks. *Pearl* and *Tryal* emerged first into open sea, then *Centurion* with *Gloucester* close on her quarter and *Severn* and *Wager* with the little *Anna* pink following in their wakes. The dreaded Straits Le Maire had been passed in two hours, and with much less trouble than would have been experienced coming up Spithead.

As *Centurion*'s bows came level with the cape, Dennis, her third lieutenant, let his Irish blood overcome his awe of the Commodore.

"The Pacific Ocean!" he yelled, jumping into the mizzen-shrouds and waving his hat. "Give it a cheer, boys!"

Down in the stinking 'tween-decks a hundred sick men, packed side-by-side in the rows of hammocks, heard the three lusty cheers. Some of them wondered listlessly what was toward; but others were beyond caring, drifting as they were in the dark passage between life and death.

THREE

The Ninety-four Days

1

It seemed to Peircy Brett that all the noise in the world was concentrated in *Centurion*'s 'tween-decks. The ship herself, a hollow wooden drum resounding to the repeated hammer-blows of giant waves, groaned and shrieked with the unremitting strain on her timbers as she was tossed high on the crests and flung down into the troughs. The hiss and roar of the seas, the high-pitched screaming of the gale, drowned any voice or footstep that might tell of activity on the sea-swept deck overhead. Even the loud monotonous clanking of the pumps, at which Brett was toiling with four seamen, a corporal of marines, and Pascoe Thomas the schoolmaster, was barely audible above the deafening uproar.

The pump-handles were cranks driving the revolving bucket-wheels of the pumps and there were four of them worked by two men each. Thus eight men could man them, and until ten minutes ago there had been eight men bending and straightening, bending and straightening, in the reeling half-darkness by the flickering light of the lantern that swung wildly from its ringbolt in the deckhead. Now only seven toiled there. The eighth lay against the bulkhead, a corpse rolling limply in the swill of filthy water; the second man that had died that night at this work.

To keep his mind from dwelling on his aching arms and soaking clothes Brett had been reckoning up the days that had passed since *Centurion* had emerged from the Straits Le Maire—into the Pacific as they had all said, he recalled bitterly. They had been days of continuous anxiety, hard work, and very little rest. From the very hour of its issuing from the western end of the Straits the squadron had been beset by weather worse than any its oldest seaman could remember. Storms of the utmost violence broke with the briefest of intervening lulls, one after another and always from the west. The seas raised by these storms were vaster than any to be encountered in northern waters, marching mountain-ranges of icy water that avalanched over the decks time and time again, drenching everything and everybody. For once the seamen, in their rare spells below, lay warmer than their officers, for whereas the deck cabins aft were deluged again and again by cascades of sea-water the hammocks swung dry; only this latter circumstance had prevented the death-toll among the sick from soaring above its normal rate of three or four a day. Others in whom the seeds of disease had taken root collapsed and were packed into the hammocks that had been occupied by the dead. The practice of sewing a dead man into his hammock had long been abandoned and the bodies were taken on deck and pitched unceremoniously overboard. There had been other losses—two hands swept overboard by a giant sea, another flung from the deck into the hold, breaking his neck. The constant strain had long ago opened the seams of the planking and made continuous manning of the pumps a vital necessity, though there were barely enough fit men to cope with the incessant demands of braces and halyards, severed cordage and split sails. Officers as well as seamen would have to work at the pumps.

Piercy Brett tried to forget the pain of his blistered hands in fixing the date when *Centurion*'s main topsail had blown clean away out of the bolt-ropes, taking a man with it. The topsail yard had been cased in ice, he remembered. That had been a week ago—no, eight days, for when this present day dawned it would be April 1st. So they had fought wind and sea and imminent death for nearly twenty-five days—fought a losing battle. For Brett had learned from Whipple the master that yesterday's reckoning made their position twelve miles due south of Staten Island and slightly *east* of it. East of a spot from which they had sailed westward more than three weeks ago! Undoubtedly there was an easterly drift helping the gales from the west to set them back. Would it ever yield sufficiently to let them get past the tip of the Horn? They could not, he thought, endure for many more days.

The unending rhythm of the crank-handles set phrases pulsing reiterant in his mind, accented with each down-thrust on the handle. *Twenty-five DAYS. How many MORE? Twenty-five DAYS. How many MORE?* He found himself gasping the words aloud and stopped abruptly, though they could not have been heard in the clamour of ship and sea. Soon, now, Saumarez would send eight hands below to relieve them, and not before it was time. Pascoe Thomas, labouring beside him, was a big man and strong but Brett knew he was nearing exhaustion; the schoolmaster's muscles were unaccustomed to such work. And there was a man short.

Men had collapsed at the pumps before now, and the first lieutenant had posted three of the ship's boys (there were twenty-one still alive) to remain by the pumps as messengers. One of the shivering lads had been pitched from the corner where they were huddled, a sudden roll of the ship hurling him against the bulkhead and partly stunning him; and Brett had thereupon ordered all three of them away to their hammocks. Thomas, who was in charge of them, had nodded his approval. But it had meant working on short-handed, for another man could not be spared to leave the pump-handles.

Brett made himself think of that day in the Straits Le Maire when all seemed to be going so well. He had dry clothes on then and a hot breakfast inside him. Already it seemed infinitely long ago; even the lull yesterday morning, before the present storm had risen in its fury, was far in the past. It might have been a week, not twenty-four hours, since *Centurion*'s longboat had succeeded in reaching *Gloucester*, though he could picture vividly the boat, with its crew pulling desperately at the oars, soaring high and disappearing over the enormous ridges of the waves. She had taken the carpenters to assist in the speedy repair of the other ship's broken mainyard. After that there had been just time to send a spare pump to *Tryal*, whose own pump could not keep pace with the rising flood in her hold, before the gale had freshened and grown to a full storm. All her six consorts had been sighted by *Centurion* during that lull. He wondered whether all six were still afloat after the terrible night that was now passing into morning.

Dark shapes came staggering into the dim lantern-light. Relief at last! Brett relinquished his crank-handle to someone (he thought it was Louis Leger, the French seaman who had replaced Bussey, now dead, as cook-steward to the Commodore) and groped for his tarpaulin coat. He had the forenoon watch-on-deck so he could snatch a couple of hours' rest on the damp palliasse of his cot. At the last moment he remembered the dead man and with a nudge and gesture directed two of his weary pump-mates to bear the body up on deck and throw it overside. Then he clawed and clung his way up the ladders to the storm-swept deck.

As he heaved himself from the hatchway on to the deck planking he was buffeted, blinded, and almost swept off his feet all in the same moment. Recovering his balance (it was a flood of sea-water pouring aft that had taken him off balance) he saw that a pallid ghost of daylight was beginning to make visible the fearsome picture of a ship fighting for her life. Masts and spars bare of canvas reeled wildly against the black clouds; a double-reefed mizzen-topsail to keep her from broaching-to was all she could carry. Spars and rigging showed a dull gleam of ice in the wan light, and thick snowflakes whirled in eddies while she wallowed in the troughs of the great grey waves that leaped above her or drove horizontally when she rocked dizzily to their crests. The still air down below and the ceaseless labour at the pumps had warmed him, but up here the icy wind chilled him in a few seconds. Lifelines had been rigged shoulder-high along both sides of the upper deck; Brett was clutching one now, and it was frozen to an iron-like stiffness. He could just discern a dark mass of men crouching and toiling up in the bows and thought he could make out Saumarez's tall form there. Probably they were yet again adding to the securing ropes of the for'ard guns; if one of those worked loose on its wheeled carriage it could do as much damage to the ship as a well-aimed enemy shot.

A mighty wave leapt yardarm high and toppled its crest on to the foredeck as Brett started to work his way aft along the lifeline. The surge of water overtook him but he was ready for it and clung to the slippery lifeline while it subsided. The thigh-length leather seaboots he was wearing were a godsend in these conditions; but he thought of the men in Saumarez's party and shivered inwardly. Those men could not have an inch of dry clothing on them and most of them would be barefoot as their custom was. The toughest of seamen could not long survive when there was no respite from icy water and freezing wind.

He reached the helm. Beyond the dark figures of the two tarpaulin-clad quartermasters stood another, erect and unsupported, swaying easily to the violent motions of the ship. It stepped forward and a hand gripped Brett's arm.

"Go for'ard, Mr Brett, if you please," said the Commodore's calm voice, very close to his ear. "Tell Mr Saumarez to call the watch below and send his men down."

"Aye, sir," shouted Brett, and started to go back along his lifeline.

So Anson was aware of the danger of losing men from mere prolonged exposure to intense cold in soaked clothing. Likely enough, though, the Commodore considered them just as he would consider a length of cordage

71

that must be taken out of use before it broke with continual chafing. All this time, all these twenty-five days, he had driven men and officers to the limits of their strength, until the men cursed him under their breaths (Brett had heard them and said nothing) and Lieutenant Dennis had called on every saint in the Romanist calendar to soften his commander's heart or send him to sleep for one whole day. But Anson, so far as Brett had observed him, took no sleep at all. And if he had not driven them, he suddenly realised, *Centurion* would not now be lifting staunchly and reassuringly under his staggering feet.

He reached the foredeck without encountering more than flung spray from the wavecrests, located Saumarez and yelled his message. The first lieutenant's answering shout was partly lost in the blast and howl of the wind.

"You relieve . . . eight bells morning watch . . . get some rest."

Brett released one hand to wave acknowledgement and hurriedly clutched the lifeline again as *Centurion* bucked like a horse. He began his lurching journey aft, noting the growing light in the east and the quite unwarranted stimulation it brought to his drooping spirits. He was dog-tired. The thought of letting himself collapse on that wet, smelly palliasse in his cabin was like a vision of heaven. Then he saw the wave.

At first he took the long dark wall far out to larboard for a low headland of rock-reef and his heart jumped into his mouth. Then he saw that it was moving, racing towards *Centurion* as smoothly as a ruler moved across a chart. When the ship soared to a crest he could see that it filled the whole horizon, a wall of water so huge that it dwarfed the tremendous waves between it and the ship. All along its crest was a smoke of wind-blown water, and as it came nearer the long white streaks of foam on the dark-green slope appeared like snow-gullies on the precipices of a mountain-range.

Brett had stopped moving when he first saw the great wave. He was motionless, clinging to the frozen rope,

72

when it struck the ship—not on the beam, which must inevitably have overwhelmed her, but on the larboard quarter. The dark mountain of water reared high above the poop, seemed to hang there against the clouds for a moment of time, and then crashed down with a cataclysmic shock and roar. He felt *Centurion* reel and the deck beneath him sink under the weight of water. The whole of the poop was lost beneath the waterfall that submerged stern and after-deck. Brett saw a tossing flood charging towards him and hung on for dear life, instinctively closing his eyes. The water tore at his body for a full ten seconds before he felt it slacken and subside, chilling him to the bone and convincing him for one dreadful moment that the ship had foundered. When he could see again he found himself hanging by his hands with his boots slithering on a steeply-tilted deck as *Centurion* heeled far over to starboard. The swirling flood was pouring from her decks over the rail, taking with it pieces of splintered wood. Slowly, slowly she righted herself, and before she had regained an even keel Brett had seen that the helm was deserted, the wheel spinning.

He hurled himself aft with little care now for the lifeline and grasped the flailing spokes in the same instant that another man, rising from the deck where he had been hurled by the wave, took hold of the wheel from the other side. Together they brought *Centurion*'s bows round until the wind was on her starboard bow. Only when she was soaring and falling as before did Brett glance at his companion. It was a second or two before he recognised the face, dripping water and streaked with lank wet hair, as that of the Commodore. Anson's crisp voice pierced the tumult of the elements.

"She'll do, Mr Brett. If she survived such a sea as that she'll survive anything."

It was light enough now to see his faint smile and the gleam in his eyes. As they strove together at the wheel, holding her against the powerful thrust of the seas, men began to come aft along the lifelines by twos and threes, among them one of the quartermasters.

"Where's your mate?" Anson demanded.

"Overboard, sir, I reckon," panted the man.

Anson raised his voice. "Mr Saumarez! Find me a quartermaster and send him here to the wheel. Hand over to this man," he added to Brett. "Go and get some sleep if you—"

"Commodore, sah!" It was Ham, leaping down like an ape from the poop-deck. "Big smash, sah—quarter-gallery gone smash-oh, sah!"

"Very well," said Anson coolly. "You may go and see what's happened, Mr Brett. If the damage is well above waterline don't trouble to report to me. We can do nothing about it until this gale moderates—as I expect it to do before sunrise."

With Ham's lanky figure leading the way Brett made for the after-cabins below the poop-deck. The great wave had expended the main force of its blow on the angle of the high stern; and the evidence of that force was plain to see. The wooden rail and framing of the larboard quarter-gallery had gone, only a few jagged splinters remaining to show where it had been. The massive gilded carving that ornamented stern-rail and gallery had vanished, torn away as by some monstrous claw, and the windows of the cabin giving on to the gallery had been smashed in, frames and all. Water had poured through the cabin and left a mess of sodden clothes, bedding, books and other articles piled against the bulkhead. It was Saumarez's cabin; Brett's was next to it.

Staring out across the waste of huge tossing waves, Brett saw that morning had come, a ghastly pallor reaching across below the clouds. He leaned perilously outboard and decided that the damage had been confined to the upper part of the stern, well clear of the wavecrests that surged below him. He would take Anson at his word.

The deluge that had poured in through the gap had not entirely spared his own cabin and water gleamed in puddles and runnels everywhere. His cot, slung from the deck-head beams, was soaked and water was still dripping from the planking above it. Choosing a corner that seemed clear of the worst drips, he flung his wet palliasse down and stripped off his seaboots and tarpaulin. He fell rather than lay down on the palliasse; and soaked and chilled though he was, fell instantly into the uneasy sleep of exhaustion.

2

"I want you to check all your figures very carefully, Mr Whipple," said Anson. "Use the chart-room and take your time."

He pointed to the door of the chart-room, which opened off the stern cabin where he was sitting at the table. Whipple, the master, a grizzled man whose bony face wore a perpetual expression of anxiety, hesitated.

"I assure you, sir, that I've already—"

"Do as I say, if you please," said the Commodore.

Whipple grunted something that might have been an *Aye, sir*, and went to the chart-room, balancing himself with some difficulty against a sudden heave of the cabin deck as *Centurion* hoisted her stern on a wave. Anson rescued a rolled chart that had fallen from the table and sat back in his chair with a sigh. He could relax for a minute or more, and that was a rare luxury these days. The fact that no gale was blowing, so that the big waves over which the ship was climbing and falling were not breaking, was another rarity; as, also, was the steady wind that allowed her to hold her course under main and topsails. A landsman might consider the lowering skies and high green seas to be rough weather, but compared with what the squadron had experienced during the past five weeks this was practically a calm.

Five weeks. Thirty-eight days, to be exact, for this was April 14th. Since the day when the great wave had smashed the quarter-gallery there had indeed been other

75

gales; but none had been so savage, and in the lulls between them the quarter-gallery had been stoutly repaired and the rest of his ships had been able to patch up the worst of their damage. Anson's lips tightened and the two vertical furrows between his eyebrows deepened. He knew that all the ship repairs were temporary and therefore weak. *Wager*'s jury mizzen-mast and topsail yard, *Anna*'s sprung bowsprit and *Tryal*'s leaky hull, could not be put properly to rights until they could find safe harbourage, and though there was a coast just over the northern horizon it was the coast of Tierra del Fuego and Cape Horn, which no mariner in his senses would even approach within five miles. Not until he reached the island of Socorro would there be a chance of rendering all seven vessels seaworthy again. And all of them must be far from sound. If *Centurion*, launched only eight years ago, had opened her seams in the gales, what of the much older *Gloucester* and the overladen *Anna*?

And there were the men. What was left of them. *Centurion*'s complement, the number of hands essential to her efficient handling under all conditions, was 400; he could muster something short of 250, and only a very few of those were topmen capable of laying aloft in a gale. The other ships must be shorthanded in similar proportion. As in his own case, their captains would be using officers, cooks, carpenters, marines—any human being on board that could stand erect—to man halyards and braces. It was, Anson found, comforting to remember that Francis Drake, making this same passage in 1577, had called his ships' companies together and told them that he would have "the gentlemen to hayle and draw with the maryner, and the maryner with the gentlemen".

But that was in Elizabeth's time when the navy was a haphazard affair. The Royal Navy of 1741, the protégé of a Board of Admiralty that was one of the most powerful bodies in the realm, should be planning and building ships of a far more advanced design than the over-crowded hulks it seemed content with; and manning them, too, with trained seamen who would take the same pride in their skill and their Service that he himself took. Knowing what he knew of the present Board, that was merely a vain imagining, a dream. Yet the dream had come into his mind and it brought a reaction; for the first time on this voyage Anson allowed himself to feel anger and resentment. It was a part of his pride—his vanity, perhaps—to have nothing to do with excuses, to scorn any shifting of blame from himself to his superiors. If the means he was given for a task were inadequate, he would shape them into adequacy by the sheer force of his own competence and will. That he had accepted as being his duty, but it was his pride as well. Now, however, in this moment of vision, he looked beyond to the muddle and corruption that had sent him on a mission of war, through dangerous seas, with unsound ships manned by weaklings and cripples. And he was angry.

There was no time to indulge this feeling, for here came Whipple from the chart-room, and Whipple's business was of the first importance.

"Now, Mr Whipple," said Anson. "Sit down and we'll compare notes. You understand, I hope, that I entertain no doubts of your efficiency as sailing-master. In this matter, however, we have what could be called an unknown quantity, and upon that, two opinions are better than one."

"The longitude, sir," said Mr Whipple dolefully.

A pale sun, making a brief appearance three days ago, had given a noon-sight from which latitude could be calculated. But longitude had to be worked out from the dubious records of traverse-board and log; and longitude was vital in the decision now to be taken.

"Precisely," Anson said, unrolling the chart. "On latitude we are agreed, I see. Fifty-nine degrees and thirty minutes south. Your figures for the dead-reckoning?"

The master laid a large stiff-covered notebook on the table. It had been soaked by sea-water and dried, and he smoothed the creased pages with his fingers as he turned them.

"Staten Island gave us the only certain longitude we've had, sir—sixty-four degrees thirty west. Dead-reckoning gives six hundred and thirty miles westerly. I make that longitude eighty-two west, sir."

Anson, frowning, rested the point of his pencil on the chart. "What did you allow for easterly drift?"

"Average two knots, sir." Whipple shrugged his shoulders despondently. "Not much better than guesswork."

"No. My guess was three knots. That puts us in longitude seventy-eight."

Anson fell silent, deep in thought, while Whipple watched him covertly. A ship's log, measuring her speed through the water and thus giving the distance run in a given time, would record eight knots—eight sea-miles covered in an hour—though a three-knot current setting against her made the actual distance sailed only five miles. They could allow for that. But what of the many occasions when they had been forced to lie hove-to for hours, the gales when it had been impossible to cast the log, the innumerable tacks against head-winds? It was true that most of their westing from Staten Island had been made in the last fortnight, and that dead-reckoning during that period was likely to be reasonably accurate. This was not, he decided, a mere throw of the dice but a lead from a tolerably strong hand.

"Very well," he said. "Eighty-two or seventy-eight, we shall clear this Cape Noir, the western tip of the Horn, on a course laid from our present position to Socorro. You concur, Mr Whipple?"

"Certainly, sir. On your seventy-eighth parallel we'd clear it by a hundred and fifty miles. On my eighty-second, by three hundred."

Anson nodded soberly. "A lee shore and a terrible one. The more sea-room the better. Well, Mr Whipple, I shall alter course northward as soon as you've given me a course to steer. Set about it now, if you please. You may use my cabin."

"Aye, sir. Thank you, sir."

Anson left the master bending over the chart and stepped out on to the upper deck. The presence of the marine sentry outside his cabin door was symbolic of the ordered routine which had returned, thanks to the exertions of Saumarez and Brett, in place of the near-disorder occasioned by the succession of gales. The man brought his musket smartly to attention as the Commodore came out, and Anson noticed that he was a corporal.

"Your name?" he demanded, stopping.

"Thompson, sir."

"It's not customary for a man of your rank to do sentry-duty, Corporal Thompson. This was by Colonel Cracherode's order?"

" 'Twas my idea, sir. The Colonel's abed sick these last five days." Thompson, a born explainer, seized his opportunity. "There's not enough marine privates left to go round, d'ye see, sir. Sentry on powder-room, another on spirit store, reliefs every two hours. There's the pumps—"

"Very well, Corporal."

Anson lingered, eyeing the sentry curiously; and suddenly he knew the reason for his interest. Thompson's bulky form, his craggy features, and the grizzled eyebrows that overhung sunken eyes, gave him a close superficial resemblance to Lord Chancellor Hardwicke. Odd that this fellow, ill-educated and unintelligent, should be so like the cleverest man in England. Something prompted a further question.

"You're a married man, Corporal?"

"Yessir. Wife and one daughter in Portsmouth. Daughter's twenty-two, had her birthday yesterday. Time she was married. I says last time I—"

"Very well, Corporal," Anson said more sharply, cutting short the burst of loquacity which (he told himself irritably) he should never have invited.

The thought that Elizabeth Yorke could be very little older than Thompson's daughter entered his mind for a fleeting instant and was gone when he observed the second lieutenant waiting to speak to him a few paces away. Brett's ingenuous face showed his surprise; he must have overheard that conversation with Thompson. Anson made Brett wait a few moments longer while he sent a keen glance round him. The cold grey sky, the cold green seas; the six other ships all within two miles of the Commodore as he had ordered; *Centurion*'s sails—all but the fore-topsail were new canvas—drawing well with a strong wind a little before the beam; Lieutenant Dennis with a working-party up for'ard reeving new cordage on the spritsail yard. All was as it should be, and with this wind he could tack *Centurion* and lay her on that northward course.

"Well, Mr Brett?"

"I have the watch, sir," said Brett formally. "I've to report four burials this morning. Men sick in the hospital, seventy-three. But two that were sick reported for duty this morning, sir—they had scurvy and recovered from it."

"Very well. They'll be needed. Send a hand to call Mr Saumarez, if you please. My compliments and he's to come on deck. Then call up all hands."

"Aye, sir."

Anson turned to look at the ships of the squadron again. Because of the high sea that was running their hulls were never all in sight at the same time, but all would see *Centurion* make her alteration of course, an alteration of one hundred degrees. No need to call attention to it by firing a gun. The bosuns' calls were shrilling and men were coming up from below; not the jostling surge of humanity that a call for "All hands" would have brought six months ago but a thin trickle of men, listless of movement and indifferent to the blows and curses of the petty officers. There were barely enough for the simple task of laying her on the other tack. Saumarez and Brett came trotting along the deck, and here was Whipple at his elbow notebook in hand.

"I shall alter course northerly, gentlemen. Lay her on the larboard tack, if you please."

Anson found himself giving the order with weighty emphasis. This was literally the turning of a corner; the worst had been left astern, and instead of heading obliquely towards the Polar ice he was to steer for the lower latitudes, for warm blue seas and islands of plenty. He and Whipple went to stand beside the helmsman, while along the deck the hands under the lieutenants' direction slacked off and hauled in on fore, main, and mizzen braces.

"Handsomely, now," said Whipple as the wheel brought her through stays and the wind bellied out the fore staysail. "Meet her. Steady as you go. Course to sail is north a point west, sir," he added to Anson.

"Very well, Mr Whipple. Quartermaster, steer north a point west."

The helmsman, his eyes on the binnacle compass, spun the wheel a few spokes and brought it back a little.

"Course north a point west, sir."

"Make it so."

It seemed appropriate to the occasion, this time-honoured ritual of responses. Anson climbed to the poop-deck to observe the rest of the squadron. All were turning, *Anna* a little tardily. *Anna*'s bowsprit had lost its gammoning in the gales and she had to go about cannily; but then, there was not one ship without a sprung spar or weakened timbers among them. Now every ship had conformed to the new course and the squadron was headed northward, in a few weeks to reach the rendez-vous at the island of Socorro. If this wind held, broad on the larboard bow, they should make 160 miles of northing by this time tomorrow. He went down to his cabin.

And the fair wind held, though with more than one ominous lull when it backed capriciously only to blow strongly again from the same quarter. On the next morning the ships were still swooping and plunging over the huge rollers on their northward course and until mid-afternoon it continued to blow strong and steady. Bitter cold though it was, there was a lookout at *Centurion*'s foremast-head; Anson dared not put his whole trust in the imperfect chart and it was by no means impossible that some rock or island unmarked by past navigators should appear in his path.

At four bells of the second dogwatch the wind strengthened to half-a-gale and the main courses were taken in. At the same time the cold Antarctic haze with which they were so familiar spread over the darkening surges, reducing visibility to less than a cable's length.

"Keep your eyes skinned, Vokes," warned Brett as a burly seaman, bundled in layers of clothing, started up the shrouds to relieve the lookout.

"Aye, sir—but I doubt if I'll see the length of me arm."

The night had come early, helped by cloud and flying mist. Somewhere above the obscuring vapours a full moon was rising and its light, just filtering through, was sufficient to show the angry seas leaping past the ship's hull to vanish into a dark wall of haze. Brett, who had the watch on deck and was pacing back and forth in an attempt to keep the penetrating cold from his bones, halted in mid step and cocked an ear. The rush and roar of the seas, the groaning of *Centurion*'s timbers as she toiled over crest and trough, the high-pitched shrilling overhead and the rhythmic clank of the pumps below decks—the familiar noises were all that he could hear. Yet for a moment he had thought to distinguish a sound beyond them, a sound like the booming of distant cannon. He forgot it on the instant when he heard a shout from the quartermaster at the wheel.

"Wind's veering, sir—can't hold this course much longer."

"Very well." Brett swung round to the duty midshipman huddled against the foot of the mizzen-mast. "Mr Keppel, call the Commodore. Tell him I'm going to tack. Bosun there! Pipe all hands. On your feet, duty watch! Stand by those braces."

The wind was certainly veering northerly—and blowing the haze clear, too. As the watch below came tumbling up on deck the disc of the full moon showed itself through the thinning veil of cloud. Brett could watch the hands obeying his shouted orders by this growing light, see the canvas of the topsails flatten and belly out again as the wheel was put over and *Centurion* came round on the starboard tack. Suddenly the moon swam out into a patch of clear sky and the haze seemed to open ahead. Turning, Brett found the Commodore at his side. Anson opened his mouth to speak but the words never found utterance. A frantic yell from the masthead lookout checked speech and movement for a long moment.

"Land! Deck! *Deck, there!* Land on the stabboard beam! Two mile distant!"

"By God!" Brett jerked, and jumped into the mizzen-shrouds.

"Impossible!" he heard Anson exclaim behind him.

"Look, sir, look!" he cried. "A coast—breakers!"

It was lit by brilliant moonlight. A long line of black cliffs, gleaming veins of ice in the pinnacled crags above them, the white writhing of surf at the foot of the black wall. Before another word could be spoken there came another hail from the masthead, a cracked screech this time.

"Land! Land! Ahead, land right ahead! Distant three mile, sir!"

Brett craned his neck, peering below the mizzen-yard to see beyond the bowsprit. A boss of black rock showed above the wave-tops, an island or the nose of a headland. They were embayed, with the minimum of sea-room for escaping; perhaps not even that. Saumarez came running aft, his gaunt face grim in the moonlight. The Commodore's penetrating voice rang out.

"Pipe all hands! Pass the word for Mr Cargill—Mr Saumarez, I shall wear ship. See that those braces are smartly handled. Well, Mr Whipple?"

"That's—that's Cape Noir!" The master, who had

stumbled out on deck a minute before, was literally wringing his hands. "Oh, sir—oh my God—"

"That'll do, Mr Whipple," Anson said sharply. "The responsibility is mine. We shall in any case win clear." He turned to Cargill, the gunner, who had arrived panting. "Clear away number one gun, Mr Cargill, and load. I want one shot fired to leeward." Then to the quartermaster, "Stand by to go about."

It was many hours later when Peircy Brett was able to realise fully what those few minutes meant to his commanding officer. Then he could marvel at the coolness of speech and manner, the speed with which he had taken control. Anson's hopes had been shattered at a blow. Instead of leading his battered ships and decimated crews towards waters where they would have some faint hope of safety and rest he had led them into the very jaws of death. A miracle, nothing less, had saved them from complete disaster, but now they were faced with days and weeks, perhaps months, of further struggle; south once more until they could be sure they were clear of the western tip of the Horn, then west to find the start of the long passage up the coast. To Anson it must have seemed that the Expedition was doomed finally and absolutely. Yet he had shown no sign of it. Truly a man of oak and iron, Brett told himself. But George Anson, who had heard and complacently approved that description, was for the first time doubting it. In no man can self-confidence coexist with humiliation; and Anson had been greatly humiliated.

When every ship had been seen to reverse her course following *Centurion*'s example, when all the squadron was flying southward retracing the sea-miles covered so hopefully, when the veering wind had settled firmly in the north-west and there could be no doubt that the immediate danger was past—not until then did Anson go to his cabin, leaving the ship in charge of Saumarez. The attentive Ham was dismissed with a curt word. Leger the cook, hovering with inquiries about food and drink, was bidden sharply to his quarters. The Commodore sat alone at his table and confronted his failure.

The easterly drift during the passage from the Straits Le Maire had been vastly greater than he had thought possible. Whipple the master had been deceived by it too. These were excuses and he would not tolerate them. The fact remained that he had failed as navigator—had failed his ships and the men in them who had trusted to his leadership. But for God's mercy every ship and every man would now be lost, pounded to pieces on that terrible shore. A godly captain, like Blake a hundred years ago, would have mustered his ship's company to thank the Lord for the miracle of their salvation, he reflected with a wry half-smile.

George Anson was not a religious man though he conformed strictly to the religious requirements of his country and his Service. He believed in God; but he believed more strongly in himself and his good fortune. He recalled now the sudden revelation of the clearing night sky, allowing the danger to be seen in time, and the wind that had veered northerly just when he needed it to make good his escape. He had indeed failed—but luck, Anson's ally Fortune, had seen to it that he did not pay the penalty of failure.

He had been sitting with his head bowed, but now he lifted it and straightened himself in his chair. Nothing was lost. He was faced with yet another challenge, and by heaven he would meet it boldly! He shouted for his servant and the Negro came running.

"Tell Leger to bring salt beef and biscuit. And Ham—bring the madeira and a glass."

"Yass—*sah*!" said Ham, grinning happily.

3

As if intimidated by the Commodore's renewed resolution, the Horn spared its fury for the next ten days.

Moderate seas and moderate gales attended the squadron as it held on, south by west, putting league after league between itself and the dangers it had so narrowly escaped. The chance of further strengthening damaged spars and plugging the worst of the leaks was eagerly seized, officers and their depleted crews working with the doggedness of men who knew that their lives depended upon it. In *Centurion* the labour at the pumps was reduced to two hours in each watch, one or two sick men every day reached a convalescence that enabled them to undertake minor duties, and the death-roll from scurvy and other ills began to decrease. For the first time in many weeks Peircy Brett heard men singing:

> *Salt beef, salt beef*
> *Is our relief*
> *Salt beef and biscuit bread-oh*

they chanted in the stinking mess-decks, and Brett's own spirits rose in the realisation that theirs were still unconquered by misery and disappointment.

The old sailor-song was apt enough, for Anson had taken the opportunity of low seas to replenish his ships' food-stores from the storeship *Anna*. Of beef and pork pickled in brine there was ample supply, though much of if had been rendered nearly uneatable by the water that had flooded *Anna*'s hold. The "biscuit bread" was all infested with weevils but that was customary. The worst of it Anson dealt with in a manner devised by himself. *Anna* was carrying vast quantities of brandy, so he had the worm-infested bread soaked in the spirit and set on fire; when the flame was blown out they could at least (as Saumarez commented) take their meat dead and cooked instead of live and crawling.

The most serious problem was water-shortage. Anson could have wished that three-quarters of those brandy-casks had been filled with water, even if it was the stale green liquid that filled such water-casks as were left. The normal allowance of water was a gallon a head for all

86

purposes, but that had been reduced to two-thirds of a gallon as soon as it became apparent that there would be weeks, even months, of delay before they reached the island of Socorro where they expected to f d water. Now the ration had to be cut down again, to half-a-gallon; two quarts in twenty-four hours was hardly enough to satisfy a man's thirst and it meant that all cooking and washing had somehow to be managed with sea-water. Yet the natural grumbling at this deprivation was short-lived, for at the end of ten days the squadron was once more heading for those visionary islands whose crystal springs and plenitude of fruits began to haunt the dreams of more than one weary seaman.

The bearings Whipple had taken as the ships fled from the land-trap of the western Horn had convinced the master beyond all doubt that it was indeed Cape Noir, and the accurate dead-reckoning they had been able to take placed them almost on the 60th parallel and—certainly this time—well beyond longitude 80° west. With confidence Anson altered course northward. Twelve hundred sea-miles, possibly less than a fortnight's sailing, could bring them to the island so grandly named Nuestra Señora del Socorro and the end of their present troubles. But the Horn had not finished with them yet.

In the afternoon of April 24th the fresh westerly that had been blowing so steadily began to strengthen and by evening *Centurion* was hove-to under topsails only, enduring the battering of a savage storm. All night it blew with increasing fury. Morning found the ship in serious danger of capsizing, the gale laying her on her beam-ends when she rose on the crests of the mountainous waves. Every man capable of keeping his feet had been standing-by on deck throughout the night but it had been impossible, with the few able-bodied topmen that were left, to take in sail in that black darkness with *Centurion* reeling and lurching like a maddened horse. Now it had become imperative to rid her of top-hamper if she was to survive.

Anson, standing by the helm where Brett and Whipple were lending their strength to the quartermaster's, looked from the straining topsails to the men huddled below the weather rail with sheets of spray flying over them. He was hatless, his long hair streaming in the wind, and his face was as wooden and unmoved as the ship's figurehead. His voice topped the storm's.

"Hands to take in sail!"

Brett, wrestling with the wheel-spokes, drew in his breath sharply. He knew the urgent need, but he knew—as did the hands—the difficulty and extreme risk of going aloft in these terrible conditions. A few, a very few, men stood forward at the Commodore's shout. Saumarez and the surviving bosun, Tully, cuffed and cursed others to their feet. But the gale itself saved them. At the first slackening of the sheets every seam in fore and mizzen topsails was split from top to bottom, the clue and buntlines snapping like threads instantaneously and the lashing canvas shredding away until nothing was left of either sail. The main topsail remained intact, but loose as it was it thrashed with such violence that it threatened at every moment to bring down the topmast. If sail and mast went overboard in their tangle of stays and rigging it could well be the beginning of a swift end to *Centurion's* desperate struggle. Anson's voice rang again like a trumpet-call.

"I want that sail cut away. And—"

A deafening thunder of spray and wind and flailing canvas interrupted him. When it had passed his shout came more loudly still.

"I'll have none but volunteers for this task!"

Eight men sprang into the main-shrouds. Through the grey veil of spray and spindrift Brett saw them, small dark figures against the flying clouds, laying out along the mainyard. The mast was whipping back and forth in arcs so wide that the end of the topsail yard seemed almost to touch, on the windward roll, the faces of the green precipices of water that rose in succession above the

88

wallowing hull. The giant forces at work on those tiny figures, he thought, must surely catapult them from their precarious hold. The men had to stand on thin sagging foot-ropes and support themselves with one hand against the furious blast of the wind while with the other hand they used their jack-knives to cut loose the wildly-flapping sail.

Brett was aware of Anson close beside him, watching intently the struggle going on overhead.

"There are too few of them, sir," he yelled against the wind.

But as he spoke the sail began to split and flap. In a moment the canvas was rent across where the knives had ripped it and in a few seconds it was gone, torn into strips which flew away and vanished instantly into the welter of spume and spray. Clinging and clutching, eight men came down the shrouds to the deck. Anson had dashed across to the mizzen-shrouds and was supporting himself by them. He shouted back to Brett, his voice at its fullest pitch.

"Few they may be, Mr Brett, but by God, they're *seamen!*"

Brett had never heard him give a word of praise to the deck-hands before, and even now the comment had been addressed to his second lieutenant. But it was plain that Anson had taken care that the men should hear what he said; and that, for Anson, was unusual.

Under bare poles, with a scrap of canvas rigged aft, *Centurion* rode out a storm that lasted another thirty-six hours. When at last it moderated and a lookout could be sent to the masthead the exhausted men learned the worst possible news: there was not a sail in sight. *Gloucester, Severn, Pearl, Wager, Tryal,* and *Anna*—all had gone. In the ensuing days and weeks nothing was seen of them. Whether all six ships had foundered in the storm, as was likely enough, or whether they had been blown far beyond the horizon, was impossible to say. For the Commodore there was only one course—to sail on with his one remaining vessel and her enfeebled crew.

Sea and storm had no mercy for *Centurion* in her half-crippled state. April passed into May, and still the gales rose and smote her at intervals of a few days, once with the hammer-blow of a gigantic wave like the one that had all but sunk her a month earlier. She survived the ordeal, but many of her sick and dying did not. Battered and shaken in their close-packed hammocks down in the fetid atmosphere of the 'tween-decks, soaked and chilled by the water that penetrated everywhere, with nothing to be done for them except the occasional provision of bowl or bucket, the victims of disease had a minimal chance of recovery. The daily "burials" overside numbered at least five, sometimes eight, and the hammocks emptied of the dead were quickly occupied again by men new-smitten with disease. Of the veteran soldiers of the Invalid Regiment there was not a single man left alive on board *Centurion*. The dwindling remnant of the crew was now insufficient to work the ship in any but the most favourable weather, and she was forced to carry only low sails because there were not enough hands capable of going aloft; the two midshipmen, Carpenter (who had recovered from scurvy) and Keppel, went out on the yards with the seamen, but taking in sail took so long that a squall or sudden gale could have endangered the ship had she worn all the sail that she could carry. Such canvas as she had left, in fact, was very poor stuff. The spare suits of sails Anson had providently carried with him were long ago exhausted, and all day long the deck-hands and "idlers"—waisters and holders—worked away at stitching together old pieces of canvas and repairing the cordage broken by the gales. There was little spirit left in them now. A listless apathy, rather than dogged endurance, marked their daily lives in those days of early May. Brett and Saumarez, themselves fighting against inward despair, did their best with cheerful word and bearing to raise the spirits of their men; and increasingly, as the days wore on, they held out the hope of an end to this misery when Socorro Island was reached. Over them all brooded the aloof figure of the Commodore, silent and resolute.

There was one cheering circumstance to encourage them. Whether the winds blew a full gale or a moderate breeze they blew always from the west, so that *Centurion* made steady progress northward. To starboard, beyond the eastern horizon, was land, a wild and mountainous coast with hundreds of barren islands and inland glaciers, a lee shore with no help for them even if it had been possible to land there. Socorro lay close to this shore, and on May 8th the jagged snow-capped mountains of Patagonia were sighted. That evening the haggard, unwashed men crowded for'ard to stare at the goal of their hopes, Nuestra Señora del Socorro.

Under the low dark skies, across the tossing waste of dark water, the island stood higher and higher on the starboard bow until they could see its black inhospitable cliffs and the white surf leaping below them. There was not a tree, not one speck of green, to be discerned on its craggy ridges.

"Palms and tropic sunshine," murmured the Honourable Augustus Keppel to his fellow-midshipman. "Sparkling streams. Lovely Indian girls feeding us with juicy fruits."

The black fuzz of a manly beard with sundry cuts and scars showing through it was evidence of his vain attempt to shave with the aid of sea-water. Carpenter, a slight boy with cheeks hollowed by illness, summoned a feeble grin.

"Not on that bald bloody knob, Gussie," he said. "And I'll lay a hundred to one there's no landing-place."

In that Midshipman Carpenter was proved right.

Anson had *Centurion* hove-to that night, and the two succeeding days were spent in cruising back and forth in a vain search for some beach or inlet where a boat could land. There were possiblities to be guessed at with the aid of the telescope, but there was nowhere a safe anchorage for the ship in any case; undermanned as she was and dangerously slow to handle, it would have been foolhardy

91

to close that iron shore in the high seas and high winds that never ceased. On the third day, unprecedentedly, the Commodore summoned a conference of officers in his great cabin. The three lieutenants were there, Whipple the master, the chaplain Richard Walter, and Pascoe Thomas the schoolmaster. Colonel Cracherode of the marines was still seriously ill. Anson's glance went swiftly round the half-dozen men sitting or standing round his table; the patched and salt-stained clothes, the gaunt faces smirched with stubble beards.

"I don't need to explain to you our present situation, gentlemen," he said. "I shall tell you my intention and hear your comments."

His tone was level and unemotional as ever. One would never guess (thought Peircy Brett, watching him) that here was a man facing his second failure of this voyage; a leader whose own hopes, on which his followers had relied, had again been dashed to the ground.

"Socorro is useless to us as a haven," Anson went on. "Our one chance of restoring our strength lies seven hundred miles to northward. We should find at Juan Fernandez all that we are so sorely in need of."

"And that's sure!" cried Dennis the third lieutenant. "By'r leave, sir—but that's the island the fellow in Defoe's book got marooned on. Found food, drink, game—all he wanted. What was his name, now?"

"Robinson Crusoe," said Brett. "But Alexander Selkirk was the original of the story. Dover rescued him. The tale of the island's plenty is true enough, for—"

"That will do, gentlemen, thank you." The Commodore's sharp interruption called them to order. "I've said that Socorro is useless to us. But it is the rendezvous laid down for the squadron in the event of separation off the Horn. I am first at the rendezvous and I shall wait here for my other ships."

There was a shocked silence. Saumarez was the first to speak.

"Have you considered, sir, the possibility that all six of

92

them may have foundered?"

"I must assume that some or all have survived the gales, Mr Saumarez. I have decided to wait at Socorro for a further twelve days before sailing for Juan Fernandez."

Richard Walter had been waiting his chance to speak, impatiently cracking his bony fingers. He was a man by nature obsequious but his tender-heartedness emboldened him to speak out.

"Sir," he said resolutely, "I beg you to reconsider that decision. If I mistake not, this island of Juan Fernandez is a week's sail from here?"

"A week in fair weather, a fortnight or more in foul," said Anson, eyeing him steadily. "You had better allow a fortnight, Mr Walter."

"Then you doom to death men you have it in your power to save, sir." The chaplain's voice was solemn. "Sail for Juan Fernandez now and you save a score of lives. The sick are crying out for water, sir—they can't endure three weeks and more on the little they are allowed."

The Commodore was silent for a moment. There was no change of expression on his set features but his level gaze went to Whipple.

"We've enough water to last three weeks on half-ration for every man," said the master. "If it was cut to one-third for the active men more could be allowed to the sick."

"The hands are suffering enough as it is," Saumarez said angrily. "It's the men who work this ship we've to look after, not loafers lying in hammocks."

"Loafers, sir!" cried Walter, firing up. "You speak of dying men, sir! Holy Writ enjoins upon us—"

"Enough of this," Anson said curtly. "The rationing of water will remain unchanged and so will my decision. I have made you aware of my purpose, gentlemen, so that you may act in accordance with it. Mr Saumarez, you will please to make known to the hands that I shall set a course for Juan Fernandez in twelve days' time. That is all, gentlemen."

When he was alone Anson got up and began to pace

back and forth, his head bent under the low deck-beams. He had been tempted to explain the factors he had to consider in deciding on his course of action; but it was neither in his nature nor in his conception of a commanding officer's role to give explanations to subordinates. They should be able to see the problems that faced him without his telling them; and indeed in Peircy Brett's intent look he thought to have discerned some understanding. *Centurion* had arrived in enemy waters. Spanish vessels—merchant ships and warships—were likely to be encountered from now on. He had to try and increase his fighting force by waiting for the rest of the squadron to join him here, while on the other hand every day of delay meant a further weakening of *Centurion*'s feeble strength; and she was already so crippled that to sail her at all was like putting a broken-down cart-horse at a five-barred gate. So he had compromised, to wait as long as he dared at Socorro and then to make for the only haven that promised salvation. But if no ships came, and if bad weather stretched the Juan Fernandez voyage to a month as it might—then George Anson and his ally Fortune had both of them failed, finally and absolutely.

The fortnight of cruising on station off Socorro brought fierce squalls, broken spars, and at last the heart-sickening realisation that it had been time wasted. For no looked-for sails broke the southern horizon. Anson turned northward in worsening weather, for Juan Fernandez.

4

Beneath the dazzle of a cloudless sky the sea was a plain of darkest blue scintillating with the diamonds of a million little wave-tops. Out of it rose an island of smiling hills fleeced almost to their crests with dark-green forests, their lower slopes rolling gently down in terraces of brighter green dotted with clumps of trees to golden beaches where families of seals basked or rolled in the tiny waves that ran up the sand. The ship that was crawling slowly across the blue plain towards the island was under a single mainsail only, a dirty and much-patched sail; she had not hands enough to hoist more. The two men handling her wheel were a chaplain and a Commodore of the Royal Navy.

Juan Fernandez was uninhabited. Two centuries ago the mariner Juan Fernando had attempted to form a settlement but the survivors had been removed to the mainland when the Spaniards completed their conquest of Chile. Now, 500 miles from the coast and far from the Spanish trade-routes, it was visited by ships very seldom indeed; Alexander Selkirk the maroon had had to wait four years before Captain Dover, putting in there to water his ship, had rescued him in 1709. Had the original of Robinson Crusoe been watching from the wooded hills on this day, the tenth of June 1741, he would have been puzzled to account for the slowness of the ship's approach and the fact that she eventually let go her anchor a good half-mile from the island's coast, before coming in sight of the wide bay that offered her refuge. A closer view of her deck might have enlightened him.

Sixteen days of unremitting struggle with wind and wave had reduced *Centurion* to the last extremity. All her company that could stand on their feet were on deck—six foremast hands, two quartermasters, and half-a-dozen ship's boys. Her officers from the Commodore to Mid-shipman Carpenter were weak and deadly tired from lack of sleep. The sail they had managed to hoist when the last of the gales died away had to serve (since they could not muster strength to hoist more) when the weather cleared and the sea subsided and the breeze would have allowed her to carry full sail. That had been on June 9th. And that calm sunlit day, the first since they had passed the Straits Le Maire ninety-four days ago, had brought the landfall they had prayed for. As they approached the island the little group on *Centurion*'s deck gazed at it as men reprieved from Hell might gaze at Paradise, and when telescopes held in shaky hands revealed cascades of glittering water on the hillsides throats almost too dry for speech uttered a heartfelt thanks to Providence.

Anson alone was sufficiently in command of himself to note that his ship was in the grip of a strong current setting her towards the shore. Unable to get sail on her and keep her clear, he ordered the best bower anchor to be let go, and with infinite pains they contrived to anchor half-a-mile offshore and get the cutter into the water. Dennis with the four strongest hands was sent to look for more sheltered anchorage. It was eight hours before he returned with news of a fine bay beyond the next headland, unlimited water, goats grazing on the heights above. It remained only to take the ship there.

And now began a struggle as frustrating as any they had experienced in the past three months. The anchor could not be got up. There was no wind, and only a moderate current holding *Centurion* against the anchor-cable, but though every man including the Commodore manned the capstan-bars there were only sixteen of them all told and of these Ham the Negro alone preserved anything resembling a man's strength. At the end of four hours' gruelling labour they succeeded in bringing the cable "up-and-down"—the ship's bows directly above the anchor 56 fathoms below. Their failing muscles could do no more. When Anson at last gasped out the order to 'vast, heaving officers and men alike let themselves drop exhausted to the deck without a glance for the Promised Land so close on the beam.

Anson stayed on his feet, but he tottered like an old man when he went to the rail to gaze out to seaward.

"In three hours we shall have a breeze," he said through cracked lips. "We'll sail her off."

He was proved right. The breeze, a strong one, filled the single mainsail and with a strain and a jerk *Centurion* broke out her anchor. A united effort heaved in another fathom of cable, and with the best bower trailing fifty fathoms beneath her hull the ship headed into the bay Dennis had found. Anson held on until the anchor dragged, with consummate seamanship luffing-up in that instant. And at long last *Centurion* and her weary crew were in haven.

Peircy Brett, turning from the supervision of Pasco Thomas and his boys in the hauling-down of the mainsail, saw the Commodore toiling slowly up the ladder to the poop-deck, to stand there surveying the sunlit hills above him and the lawn-like terraces at their feet. Despite his own utter weariness Brett found himself wondering what was in Anson's mind at this moment of his arrival with one leaky ship and sixteen fit men in waters where every vessel was an enemy and every harbour a hostile port. He had his answer when Anson, coming to the taffrail and resting his hand on it, raised his voice.

"Mr Saumarez! I'll have the longboat overside and manned, if you please. Mr Brett, you'll take the cutter. Water-casks in both. Fill them at the nearest stream and bring them on board."

He paused. His voice, hoarse though it was, had been level and confident as always.

"We can do no more than that today," he went on. "Tomorrow I shall begin to disembark the sick."

And "begin", reflected Brett as he lowered his stiff and aching body into the waiting cutter, was the right word. There were 197 sick men on board *Centurion*.

FOUR

"To Annoy the Spaniards"

1

Peircy Brett toiled up the little path in the hot sunshine at a pace increasingly slow. He had been ashore on Juan Fernandez for more than a fortnight but had still not recovered completely from the effects of Cape Horn's fury. By the time he had reached the top of the little bluff overlooking the beach his knees were so shaky that he halted for some minutes, surveying the scene below him.

Centurion's second lieutenant was changed in appearance from the dapper young gentleman who had supervised the embarkation of the Invalids at Portsmouth nearly a year ago. He had taken off his battered three-cornered hat to let the sea-breeze cool him, revealing the gaudy bandana kerchief that was knotted round his head; wigs had gone by the board long ago. He wore a shirt open at the neck, breeches that showed many a stain though they had been washed as thoroughly as spring water could do it, and buckled shoes stuffed with grass to save wearing the one good pair of stockings he had left. His face, chest, and legs were mahogany brown.

The scene he was looking down at displayed at one glance the results of sixteen days' hard work, work that was still going on. On a grassy shelf between shore and forested hills were the rows of long tents that sheltered the sick men. Brett would not soon forget the two days of incessant labour, shared among sixteen exhausted men, of getting nearly two hundred helpless sick into the boats and

up to the tents; he and Anson had been one of the
two-man teams that carried them one by one ashore, and
twelve of their limp burdens had proved to be corpses
when at last they laid them down. But up in the groves
farther along the bay he could hear the cheerful shouting
of the men told off to collect bread-fruit from the tall
trees—forty or fifty feet, they were—that bore that most
useful fruit, and he knew that some of those men had
recovered from scurvy since they had been on Juan
Fernandez. Then, down at the water's edge, he could see
another party splashing about among what looked like a
mass of large brown slugs. They were catching and killing
young seals. Goat's flesh, in Brett's view, was preferable to
seal meat, but only one or two of the hands were fast
enough to catch the goats that roamed the heights above
the shore and one goat a day was the best they had
managed so far. A small strutting figure directing the
seal-killing by gesturing with the cane he carried, was
Colonel Cracherode, another who had recovered from
scurvy since coming ashore. Nearer to the tents blue
woodsmoke was wavering up from the copper-oven where
they were baking fresh bread from the remnant of the
flour, or perhaps roasting the bread-fruit which were in
great demand among the men who were convalescent. In
all, there must be three dozen men at work within the
lieutenant's range of vision, including the four who were
slowly rowing the cutter out from shore with full
water-casks on board. In fact, all the things he could see
were encouraging. Most encouraging of all were the two
ships, one big and one small, that rocked gently at anchor
on the blue waters of the bay.

The sloop *Tryal* had been sighted before they had
finished bringing the sick ashore, but it was a whole day
before her improvised spars and rags of sail brought her
into the bay and the Commodore heard her story of the
desperate fight with storm and disease. Thirty-four of her
small complement of hands had died; forty-seven were ill
and unable to stand; Saunders, one lieutenant, and three

seamen were all that were left to handle her when she reached Juan Fernandez. But at least, Brett reflected, they had now two ships, and unseaworthy though they were at present, the means of repairing them were at hand. It would be weeks, perhaps months, before they could be got ready for sea, because repair work and manning depended upon how many fit men became available; and the present rate of recovery—though it was encouraging that they were recovering at all—was very slow. All this depended, too, on their presence remaining undiscovered by the Spaniards. *Centurion* and *Tryal* could offer no resistance if a passing enemy warship, however small, saw them anchored in the bay.

And what, Brett asked himself, could the Commodore do with one 60-gun ship and a sloop, when at best they would have less than half their complement both for sailing and for fighting? Nothing, surely, but set sail westward across the Pacific for the Philippines and the Cape of Good Hope and England: a six months' voyage. Well, it would be long before he could attempt that, and meanwhile there were worse places to linger ashore than this paradisal island. Brett put his deplorable hat on his bandana'd head and continued his upward journey.

The narrow path he was following had been beaten out by the feet of the lookouts in the past sixteen days. Anson had selected the rocky peak three or four hundred feet above the shore as a lookout post (the men had named it Foremast Hill) and though hands could ill be spared it was manned night and day by two men, reliefs going up every four hours. The knob of rock was the end of a ridge that flanked a valley, lush with all manner of plants and fruits and flowers, running inland from above the beach. Peircy Brett liked to be up there alone and his single presence would release two men for the urgent and incessant duty of keeping the hospital tents clean and wholesome.

The metallic chink of a spade striking into earth came to his ears as he began to cross the leafy levels between the

100

bluff and the bare slopes that mounted to the top of Foremast Hill. Green lawns spread themselves here between clumps of flowering bushes and trees laden with lemons and small oranges. Brett came round a stand of cypresses to see a flat open space where the Commodore moved stooping along an oblong of newly-dug soil, dropping seeds into a furrow between planted sticks. Anson was hatless and clad in shirt and breeches like himself. He straightened up, with a hand to his back and a grunt, and nodded in response as the lieutenant doffed his hat. His brown beak-nosed face was glistening with sweat. Some distance beyond him his Negro servant, stripped to the waist, was digging another black oblong in the green turf.

"I doubt I'm cut out for a gardener, Peircy," Anson said with a smile. "My back's not made for bending."

Neither the smile nor the use of his Christian name surprised Brett now though both still had the quality of strangeness. Formality, even the rigid formality of the Royal Navy, could not long be maintained between two men working as a team for days on end, splashing through the shallows and struggling up the sand time after time, carrying the helpless sick who sometimes died in their arms. Indeed, there had been one occasion, on the second day when heavy rain was hindering the work, when the weary Anson had stumbled and dropped the legs of the man they were carrying and the equally weary Brett cursed his carelessness. That was a fortnight ago. Proper respect and the automatic "sir" were as invariable as ever with the lieutenant now, but with the Commodore "Mr Brett" became "Peircy" on informal occasions such as this.

"May I ask what you're sowing, sir?" asked Brett.

"Lettuce and carrots," said Anson, showing the small linen bags. "I've a considerable store brought from England for precisely this purpose. The soil here is far more fertile than that of the kitchen-garden at Shugborough."

"They'll not grow in time for the men to eat them, surely, sir."

Anson eyed him gravely. "Even that is not impossible. There is no telling how long we shall remain on Juan Fernandez. However, these and the peach and plum stones I shall sow among the trees yonder are to serve our countrymen who shall touch at this island hereafter. There will come a time, Peircy, when the South Sea will be free from war and thronged with peaceful trading-ships. You are going up to the lookout post?"

"Yes, sir. Relieving Vokes and Fortune."

"H'm. You can hail the shore from up there on a day like this, and I shall hear you. I want instant news of that sail if she reappears. She could be the *Gloucester*."

Five days earlier, a day of mist and squalls, the lookouts had sighted a distant ship under courses and main topsail only, but she had vanished in the mist before she could be identified and had not been seen since.

"Aye, sir," said Brett, touching his hat.

Anson went on with his sowing and the lieutenant resumed his journey. Twenty yards from the path Ham, flashing his teeth, sprang to attention with his spade in imitation of a marine and Brett waved a hand as he passed. Ham's smile had been absent for a full week, he remembered, after the cat Charlotte had been lost overboard just before they reached Socorro. Among the men who had died and were still dying in the tents down by the beach were some with whom Ham had been friendly, yet he was not so deeply moved by their deaths as by Charlotte's. He himself, Brett realised, had come to regard the daily death-toll as a commonplace, a necessity in their present mode of life; while the Commodore's interest in the number of survivors was of course merely a calculation of how many deckhands and gunners were likely to be left him in the end. No—that was not quite fair. Since landing on Juan Fernandez Anson had shown more than one sign of humanity. At Santa Catarina, for instance, he had held himself aloof from the hospital tents while here he made a daily inspection and dropped an encouraging word or two in every tent. Yes, there was a change—a small change but definite—in George Anson.

Brett had been mounting slowly through trees and bushes and now had reached the place where the path began its steeper ascent, zigzagging up a rocky ridge. The overcrowded hospital tents were still in his mind and he began to think about scurvy. Everyone believed it could not be prevented and no one really knew what caused it. There were some who thought that confinement below decks at close quarters, with consequent lack of fresh air, bred the disease; Saunders and Richard Walter were of this opinion. Since the incidence of scurvy bore heaviest on the men of the lower deck on long voyages it seemed likely enough—and yet a month ashore on Santa Catarina, with ample space and fresh air, had made little or no difference. Could it, Brett wondered, be something to do with diet? Hardtack and ship's biscuit for months on end—

A high-pitched shout from above him interrupted the lieutenant's reflections. The climbing path had brought him below a shoulder of the hill and the words of the hail could not be heard, but he glanced instinctively to his left where the huge expanse of sea stretched blue and empty to the straight horizon-line. From here he could see nothing breaking that line and quickened his pace to mount above the shoulder. Down the ridge a man came running as fast as the steepness of the descent would allow. It was Fortune, wrinkle-faced and grey-haired, with his ragged canvas drawers flapping round his knees.

"Sail, sir!" he shouted breathlessly when he saw Brett. "Ship-rigged, southerly—nary a doubt, sir, but what it's the old *Gloucester*!"

"Come back aloft," snapped Brett, and pounded up the ridge at his best speed.

Vokes was perched on the topmost knob with Dennis's telescope to his eye. Brett snatched it from him; he had no wind left for words. Yes, a three-master. Main topsail set, nothing else above the horizon—this was certainly the ship they had seen five days ago.

"She'm reachin', sir," said Vokes. "Wind's veered northerly. Freshenin', too."

"Yes," said Brett, aware for the first time of the strong breeze cooling the back of his neck.

Slowly, very slowly, she was coming hull-up. He had looked at her a thousand times from *Centurion*'s deck and he could not be mistaken. This was *Gloucester*.

"Take her a while t'close th'island," Fortune said. "There's that bl—that awk'ard current setting south—"

"Stay here, both of you." Brett thrust the telescope at Vokes. "I'll see you're relieved in half-an-hour."

He plunged recklessly down the path. Below the shoulder he saw the Commodore starting up the first zigzag.

"I heard the hail," Anson said as they met.

"It's *Gloucester*," Brett panted. "I'll swear to her, sir."

At once Anson turned and began to descend with rapid steps, the lieutenant close at his heels. In the few seconds of his rush down the hillside Brett had been thinking fast.

"Wind and current are against her," he said, speaking in jerks. "It may be days before she wins inshore. We were half-dead with thirst when we made the bay, sir. She's been at sea sixteen days longer than we had. If Captain Mitchell and his crew—"

"All this is in my mind, Mr Brett, thank you," said Anson over his shoulder, incisively.

They had reached the patch of cultivation among the trees. Ham was waiting expectantly beside the path. Anson snapped a command in Spanish, a language he often used to his servant, and the Negro leaped to fetch coat and hat from the bush where they hung. The Commodore shrugged himself into his coat, clapped his hat on his head, and strode on with the others at his heels.

Clearly those on the beach had heard the lookout's hail, for Saunders and Saumarez had mustered all available hands to await eventualities. Anson began to give his orders while he was still approaching them.

"Mr Saunders, away cutter's crew, if you please. Mr Saumarez, I want those full water-casks in the cutter, together with all the fresh fish and vegetables she can carry. *Gloucester* has been sighted, distant twelve miles, bearing—what, Mr Brett?"

Almost unconsciously Brett had noted how she bore and he thanked his lucky stars for it. "South by west a point west, sir."

"The cutter will steer on that bearing until *Gloucester* is sighted. Water and stores are to be put on board and Captain Mitchell given all possible aid."

Thirty minutes later the cutter was a tiny black speck far out on the southward blue. Those on shore watched until she vanished in the immensity of distance. Now they could only wait. And they waited for twenty days. At the end of that time the cutter had not returned and there were still only two vessels anchored in the bay of Juan Fernandez.

2

But for Anson's prompt action *Gloucester* must have been lost with every soul in her. Three-quarters of her men were dead. Of the eighty-two who were left from the four hundred that had sailed in her from Portsmouth all but a few were too ill to move and the remainder so weak from thirst and exposure that they could scarcely crawl about the deck. Only with the help of the cutter's crew had Captain Mitchell, himself barely able to hold the wheel, managed after many failures to shape a course for the longed-for island. Even then contrary winds and the baneful current held him for three days within sight of the bay, and it was the extra hands sent out in *Centurion*'s longboat that enabled her at last to come in and anchor beside her sister-ships of the depleted squadron.

Mitchell's story of the gales that had driven him far to

the westward, of sprung masts and broken spars and no possibility of repairing them with his little crew of dying men, made Crusoe's tale of endurance sound like a story for children, thought Peircy Brett. But indeed he had little time in the ensuing weeks for any sort of thinking that did not concern some urgent task; nor did any man on Juan Fernandez who was able to stand upright. While it seemed probable that the arrival of three British warships in the Spanish Pacific had so far passed unnoticed by the enemy, Anson dared not assume this. To render his vessels seaworthy again, to wrest from the all-devouring scurvy enough hands to man them, or one of them at least, were the twin aims for which he organised and planned. Through July into August the able-bodied men and their officers toiled at the overhauling and repair of the ships and the care of the sick. Working in watches as on shipboard allowed rest and leisure, and it was easier and more recreative leisure than they had experienced in all the twelve months past; so that those who recovered from the scurvy rapidly regained their full strength.

"There's this to be said, Peircy," said Saumarez on one occasion. "When we've buried the last to go we'll have left with us the finest set of hands that ever sailed these seas."

Brett had to admit the truth of this while privately he was still shocked at the wastage of lives. With some exceptions, it had been the weaklings that had succumbed to the disease and the constitutionally strong that had survived. Yet it could not be denied that hundreds of poor fellows now at the bottom of the sea or buried on the islands, pressed men of poor physique, would have developed into strong and healthy seamen had they escaped the scurvy. That its onset could be prevented was uncertain; it was certain that some men could and did recover from it, and Brett was convinced that the conditions in which they lived aboard ship both assisted the spread of scurvy and obstructed recovery. The increased rate of recovery and the steady lowering of the

106

death-rate after they had been six weeks ashore on Juan Fernandez supported this theory, though he still clung to the idea that fresh food in place of salt meat six months in cask had something to do with it too.

On a fine Sunday in August, the 16th of the month, Brett discovered that others besides himself were pondering the problem of scurvy. He had paused on the bluff above the beach on his way down from Foremast Hill (where two lookouts were on watch night and day as usual) to observe the busy scene below. Parties were at work on all three ships anchored in the bay and the sound of hammering and sawing came clearly across the rippled water. On the shore, above high-water line, a forge had been set up and the smiths were banging away at the making of new chain-plates and other replacement ironwork, their furnace fed by relays of men carrying wood from the pile which other men were adding to as branches were chopped up. On the green shelf above the shore the line of hospital tents had been replaced by half-a-dozen crude huts thatched with leaves, for every inch of canvas was needed for making sails. One or two figures could be seen lying beside the huts or limping slowly with the aid of sticks—invalids on the road to full recovery. The six huts housed fewer sick men than the hospital party had ever had to cope with, for the scurvy was at last relinquishing its hold. In the last three days, as Brett knew, there had been only three deaths. He was on the point of continuing his descent when he became aware of voices on the hillside below him. Pascoe Thomas and the chaplain, coming up the path, halted just out of sight of Brett to pursue an argument.

"I tell you, Mr Walter," said the schoolmaster, puffing somewhat, "that I've observed this precisely. Those of our patients that will drink the fruit juices I press for them recover. Those that can't stand the bitterness and prefer water, die. I regard that as proof positive—"

"Your observation may be precise, Mr Thomas, but your statements are not," Walter interrupted severely. "I will grant that the juice of lemon or orange may have a medicinal value, but I know of three men who never took any drink but water during their sickness and now are recovered and back at their duty. I speak of Turnbull, Binns, and O'Malley."

"All of whom had but a mild dose of scurvy," Thomas retorted. "Strong as an ox, every one of 'em. They'd have got well anyhow. Now Cowley, *Gloucester*'s gunner, was given lemon-juice repeatedly from the hour he was brought ashore. He recovered. So did Wills, and Bonny, and Holman—"

"All of whom had but recently taken the disease," the chaplain broke in sharply. "*Gloucester*'s sick were all given fruit juices, let me remind you, and at least half of them died nevertheless. Mr Ettrick will confirm me in this."

"A gross exaggeration!" shouted Thomas. "As for Ettrick, he's a numskull, a necromancer, a common ignorant leech! I will maintain, sir, in your teeth, sir—"

"Good morning, gentlemen." Brett, thinking it was time he intervened, had come towards them down the path. "I chanced to overhear some words of your argument. I found the matter of it interesting."

"The matter's of the first importance, Mr Brett," said the schoolmaster with a sulky glare at Walter. "The lives of the King's servants could depend on it."

"There at least I will agree with you," Walter said pacifically. "The man who died yesterday, Mr Brett, brought the number of dead in those three ships yonder, since leaving England, to six hundred and twenty-six—six hundred and twenty-six! All but a few of them died from scurvy."

"Aggravated, you may say, by long fatigue and the inclemency of the weather," suggested Thomas with less acrimony.

"Doubtless, doubtless. I cannot believe, Mr Brett, that God would send scurvy among us without the provision of some antidote or preventive. But when Mr Thomas here claims, on evidence that is, to say the least, of doubtful

108

accuracy—"

"From what I overheard of your talk," the lieutenant cut in hastily, "it would almost seem that these fruit juices you speak of are effective when scurvy has taken only slight hold on a man. They're—less effective, shall we say, when the disease is far advanced."

Thomas and Walter seized on this idea and began to debate it with noisy energy. Brett found himself recalling the chaplain's phrase "antidote or preventive" in conjunction with his own theory that the lower deck's diet induced the onset of scurvy. Suppose these fruit juices, which appeared to be beneficial only in the early stages of scurvy, were not antidotes but preventives. Suppose—

"That was the lookout's hail," Thomas said suddenly, breaking off his argument with the chaplain.

Brett had heard it too, a faint high call like a seagull's cry: "Sa-ail ho!"

"Down to the beach, gentlemen," he said sharply, and led the way at a brisk trot.

The ever-present threat of a surprise visit from a Spanish warship had been prepared for during the past weeks. Anson had concentrated his man-power on *Centurion*'s repairs and she was now able to fire her broadsides. With a spring on her cable, she could be turned to cover the whole entrance to the bay, and the drill for manning her in emergency had been practised so that every man knew his duty. As Brett and his two companions came down to the foreshore the bosuns' calls were shrilling, the hands were falling-in at positions marked by the petty officers, and the boats were being made ready to put off. Saumarez, Saunders, and Dennis were supervising the preparations while Anson conferred with Mitchell. This was the first time since *Gloucester*'s arrival that a sail had been sighted from Foremast Hill, and the grins and excited mutterings of the men showed that the prospect of action was far from unwelcome. The raucous cries of myriads of seabirds wheeling overhead against the blue sky, disturbed from their daily gorging of seal entrails, mocked the hoarse screeching of Colonel Cracherode at his marines, now reduced to a total force of thirteen.

Brett, hurrying to report to the Commodore, was overtaken and passed by a scraggy seaman racing down the shingle. The man, breathless with exertion, stopped in front of Anson and knuckled his forehead in salute.

"It's—*Anna*, sir," he panted. "Sure's I'm—standin' 'ere, sir."

Anson swung round. "Mr Saunders! Belay all, if you please." He turned to the seaman. "If you're mistaken, my lad, you'll pay for it. How do you know it's *Anna*?"

With an effort the man regained his breath. "Not me, sir—Parsons. On lookout with me. Transferred from *Anna*, 'e was. Know 'er anywheres."

"Very well. Make your report properly."

"Aye, sir. Bearin' due south, ten or twelve mile an' comin' up fast under all sail. Three-master but a little un."

"All sail, you say?"

"All sail to the t'garns, sir."

Brett, watching the Commodore's expressionless face, saw the pale-blue eyes widen and gleam. This news, if it was true, must be of most vital importance to Anson. His store-ship approaching at speed and carrying full sail meant that she was in better case than the rest of his ships—that the Expedition that had been in the forefront of his mind for more than a year would receive the supplies which made the difference between advance and retreat. From the hilltop above the lookout hailed again, and though the only distinguishable word was the name of the ship the men heard it and broke into a ragged cheer.

"Silence, there!" Anson roared, and turned to the commander of *Tryal*. "Mr Saunders, all parties will remain ready to embark, but at ease. Mr Saumarez, go aloft, if you please, and confirm this report."

But there was little doubt in anyone's mind that the newcomer was indeed *Anna*, and so it proved. Before Saumarez had come down from Foremast Hill she was

110

hull-up from the beach. Soon she was rounding to her anchor beside the other three ships, and that evening her adventures were made known to all.

It was two months since *Centurion* and *Tryal*, in dire straits, had barely managed to reach Juan Fernandez. *Anna*'s arrival with all her masts standing and not one case of scurvy on board was explained by her master, Gerrard. After the April gale that had scattered the squadron, *Anna* had suffered a pounding as severe as the rest had undergone, battling for three weeks with fierce winds and violent seas and losing man after man from scurvy or exposure. At the end of that time she had been driven on to a coast of inhospitable crags where the exhausted crew had given themselves up for lost. By a miracle, the little ship had been borne into an inlet where she found anchorage in twenty-five fathoms in a fine natural harbour enclosed by forest'ed mountains, and here she had remained for two months while her company slowly recovered their health and with infinite toil effected the innumerable repairs that were necessary. Fresh fish and edible green plants had supplemented the cargo of stores which they could draw on without stint, and at last Gerrard and his sixteen surviving men had been able to shape a course to the rendezvous. The pink being small and no warship, their number was just sufficient to enable them to handle her with all her sails set.

And now the bay of Juan Fernandez hummed with new and purposeful activity, the result of a council to which the Commodore had summoned the captains of *Tryal* and *Gloucester* and the master of the *Anna*. In three weeks' time, Anson told them, he expected to begin his South Sea campaign against the Spaniards; he was confident that all four ships could be made ready for sea by then. Saunders and Mitchell agreed enthusiastically, Gerrard more cautiously; and later that day Anson received a formal written request from the merchant captain that a thorough inspection should be made of his ship, which he believed to be in bad condition. Gerrard's belief was in the nature of an understatement. The survey made by the naval carpenters revealed that *Anna*'s hull was on the point of falling apart. Twelve of her beams were broken, her timbers were rotting, and all her ironwork was rusted beyond repair. An adequate refit being totally impossible, Gerrard's proposal (on behalf of his owners) to sell her to the Navy for £300 was accepted by Anson and the work of breaking up the pink was added to the incessant labour of rigging and caulking the three warships. *Anna*'s small armament—four 6-pounders, four 4-pounders, and two swivels—was taken out of her, her foremast was converted into a new mainmast for *Tryal*, and such of her rigging and canvas as was fit to use was distributed among the other ships. Her crew were sent to *Gloucester*, who was sorely in need of hands, Gerrard being appointed temporary sailing-master.

Those last two weeks of August saw the last deaths from scurvy. When the calm summer days passed into September there were barely a dozen men still lying in the hospital huts and those were on the way to recovery; Pascoe Thomas confided to Peircy Brett that this happy state of things was due entirely to the repeated doses of lemon-juice he had personally administered to the patients. Walter, who had been required by the Commodore to make a strict accounting of all the squadron's personnel, numbered a total of 335 men and boys—less than the complement required to man *Centurion* efficiently even when *Tryal* and *Gloucester* were left without any crews at all. Of these, 214 were men of *Centurion*'s original crew. The Commodore ordered his first lieutenant to prepare a watch-bill for a crew of 234, including ten men from *Tryal* and ten from *Gloucester*.

"It's blown to blazes we'll be if we meet Pizarro and his ships," Dennis prophesied to Brett when he heard of it. "Ten's a gun-crew for a 24-pounder and we've two dozen guns in a broadside. That leaves minus six hands to work the ship while we're engaged."

"Well, they're all prime seamen now, plus or minus,"

returned Brett with a grin.

"You'd not be laughing, Mr Brett, if you had my foredeck party," said the third lieutenant dolefully. "Six men, that's all I'm given. And two of those are boys."

Brett laughed again at that; but inwardly he wondered at Anson's temerity. The Commodore, he knew, intended to make a preliminary cruise in *Centurion* with the intention of taking prizes. He would have to take his perilously undermanned ship eastward towards the coast, towards Valparaiso to which Spanish merchant vessels from Valdivia, Callao, and Paita would be plying. If any suspicion of his presence had reached the Spanish Viceroy at Lima, or for that matter the Governors and Royal Officers at the smaller ports, there would be fighting-ships watching expectantly for this impudent enemy; and if Admiral Pizarro's squadron was in the Pacific as was not unlikely *Centurion*'s chances, manned at half-strength as she was, were much as Dennis had assessed them. The Commodore was no doubt doing his duty as he saw it, obeying the orders he had been given. But the thing was a desperate gamble just the same, and Brett marvelled that he himself felt no qualms or doubts about its outcome. His confidence, he decided, must have been caught from Anson. The Commodore had confidence enough for a score.

By September 7th all three ships were ready for sea. On the evening of the 8th, there being no wind, all the boats available were used to tow *Centurion* out of the bay, amid cheers from *Tryal* and *Gloucester*. And the next morning the topgallant masts were sent up, every stitch of canvas hoisted, and a course set eastward.

3

"I have rarely tasted a more excellent wine, señor," said Don Manuel Zamorra, setting down his half-empty glass and eyeing warily the Englishman who was his host and captor.

"It is kind of you to say so, señor," said Anson.

His glance strayed to the stern-cabin window, through which he could see the Spanish ship he had taken yesterday paralleling *Centurion*'s course a quarter of a mile away. He could have replied that the wine was Don Manuel's own, having been taken from the locker in the Spanish captain's cabin, but it was not George Anson's way to add to a prisoner's distress.

"Your vessel being a prize of war, señor," he went on, "you will understand that it is my duty to examine everything I find on board her, including these." He indicated the pile of papers on the table before him. "I much regret that I have had to read your private letters."

Don Manuel's thin narrow-browed face showed a momentary frown; then he raised one shoulder in a lopsided shrug. *"Es la guerra,"* he said resignedly, and drank the rest of his wine.

Anson refilled the Spaniard's glass. "Yet war need not prevent the usages of courtesy between gentlemen," he said, hoping that his rusty Spanish was striking the note of casualness he wanted. "My knowledge of your language is not what I would wish it to be, and there are in these papers a few small matters which I would ask you, of your kindness, to clarify."

The "small matters" were in fact of immense importance to the safety of his Expedition; but that Don Manuel possessed intelligence enough to perceive that importance he was inclined to doubt. He took up a paper.

"I had hoped to have the privilege of engaging your gallant admiral Don José Pizarro," he said mendaciously, "but from this letter I gather that he is not in these waters. Perhaps, however, my lamentable ignorance of your language has misled me. If you would be gracious enough to confirm—"

Don Manuel, assisted by his own wine, was gracious enough to confirm it and add other useful information. When, after half-an-hour's conversation over the cap-

114

tured papers, he was returned to his quarters under guard in Saumarez's cabin, Anson had much to think about.

It was on the fourth day after leaving Juan Fernandez that *Centurion* had sighted a big ship fifteen miles away on the weather-bow and had given chase. With the possibility that she was a Spanish warship in mind, the Commodore had cleared for action and prepared for a desperate battle; but after nearly losing her in a prolonged rain-squall they had come up with her to find that she was a merchantman and only lightly armed. Four shots fired into her rigging had been sufficient to make her bring-to. She was the *Nuestra Señora del Monte Carmelo*, captain Don Manuel Zamorra, bound for Valparaiso with twenty-five passengers and a cargo of wrought plate and silver dollars worth £18,000 in English money. Her captain, officers, and passengers had been brought off into *Centurion* and Saumarez appointed to command the prize with a small prize-crew; some of her crew of fifty-three, black men and white, were willing to go on working the ship under her new masters and the rest were confined below decks with a couple of marines to guard them. *Centurion*, Peircy Brett again taking over as first lieutenant, had at once sailed with her prize for Juan Fernandez, where they expected to arrive next day.

Sitting at his cabin table, with Don Manuel's empty wine-bottle confronting him beside the papers he had taken from the *Carmelo*, Anson was already planning his campaign on the basis of the information he had acquired. Beyond the for'ard bulkhead of the cabin, part of the duty watch was at work scrubbing the deck-planking; a man was whistling between his teeth, not untunefully, and a burst of laughter brought a shouted reprimand from the petty officer in charge. The hands were in high spirits, and no wonder with the prospect of prize-money before them. The first victorious encounter with the enemy would have vastly heightened their confidence, too, easy though the victory had been. His

115

little sloop *Tryal* with her eight guns, Anson reflected, could have taken the *Carmelo* just as easily. And *Tryal* should go a-hunting as soon as his two ships were back at Juan Fernandez. Fortune, as staunchly his friend as ever, had presented him with a chance that had to be seized with the least possible delay.

The information that the captured papers and Don Manuel between them had given him was the clearest possible evidence of Fortune's favour. Six months ago Pizarro's squadron had been beaten back from Cape Horn with the loss of two ships; the surviving vessels had returned to the River Plate in so battered a condition that a year would be required to refit them. Not knowing whether any of the British squadron had succeeded in rounding the Horn, the Spanish admiral had sent messengers across the continent to the Viceroy at Lima urging immediate action to discover and capture any intruders, to which the Viceroy had responded by equipping and despatching four large warships to patrol the seas round Juan Fernandez. And those ships, patrolling until it was deemed impossible that Anson could have reached the Pacific, had left the area on June 6th. *Centurion* had made her landfall of Juan Fernandez on the 9th. Had she arrived only three days earlier, the battered ship would have fallen an easy prey to the Spaniards, and all her company from the Commodore downwards would now be dead. For, if Don Manuel was to be believed, the Viceroy had given orders that every man without distinction was to be put to the sword.

Anson hesitated to credit this last item of news. But it did at least explain the extreme terror of all on board the *Carmelo* when they learned who was their captor, and their almost hysterical relief when they found that they were to be treated with humanity and justice. The Commodore had given strict orders that the men of *Carmelo*'s crew, whether black or white or Indian, were to be treated exactly as though they were members of his own crew, and that none of their personal belongings

116

were to be taken from them.

There was one additional piece of information that Don Manuel had supplied: the Viceroy's squadron had encountered such violent storms on their way home that they were at present laid up in Callao for a refit which would take at least two months. For two months, then, the sea-power of Spain in the South Sea was in abeyance, and Anson with his weakened force had a chance of carrying out his mission to "annoy and distress the Spaniards". Two months. But why should it not be more? Anson remembered *Anna*'s 4-pounders, now on shore at Juan Fernandez. *Carmelo* could be fitted with those. She was a poor ship with her cotton sails and weak rigging, but mount guns in her and she would be a fighting-ship of sorts. He had long abandoned hope of ever seeing *Wager* and *Pearl* again; if they had not foundered they had been beaten back from the Horn in so bad a state that they could make no second attempt to round it. But with *Carmelo* he would have four warships to oppose to the four at Callao if they came out to challenge him, and though with his inadequate crews this was only the appearance of equality it was enough to decide him.

Anson went to his sleeping-cabin and took from a locked chest the document headed "*Signed: George R.*" The "Instructions for our trusty and well-beloved George Anson, Esq." contained a great deal of matter hardly pertinent to its subject (some over-wordy government clerk had no doubt given full rein to his quill) and some of the rest was rendered so by his present situation, but the two passages that must be the groundwork of his plan were easily found for he had read them often:

> *In case you shall find it practicable to seize, surprise or take any of the towns or places belonging to the Spaniards on the coast, that you may judge worthy of making such an enterprize upon, you are to attempt it.*

That was plain enough despite the clerk's ridiculous trio of verbs concerning what he was to do to the towns. And the other, though more cautious in tone, was a clear indication of something their greedy Lordships would dearly love him to do:

> *If you shall find no occasion for your staying longer in those seas, and shall judge it best to go to the northward as far as Acapulco, or to look out for the Acapulco ship, which sails from that place to Manila at a certain time of the year and generally returns at a certain time also, you may possibly, in that case, think it most advisable ...*

Setting aside the *if* and the *may* and the *possibly*, he was to capture the Acapulco ship if he had half a chance of it. Every sea-captain knew of her, the richest treasure-ship in the world.Once a year the galleon crossed the Pacific from Mexico to Manila in the Philippines laden with silver in coin or bullion, the spoil of the New World. At Manila, the great market-port of the East, the treasure was banked or exchanged for the goods and furnishings required by the wealthy colonists of Chile and Peru. To make a prize of such a vessel would be to assure himself of fame and promotion no matter what success or failure had attended his other projects—and nothing could possibly cause the Spaniards more distress and annoyance. He locked up the document again and got out his imperfect charts of the western coast of South America. Fair winds from Mexico to Manila would be encountered in February and March, and it was now mid-September. He could spend the next four or five months working northward up the coast and doing what damage he could; Acapulco on the Mexican coast was not far short of five thousand miles from Juan Fernandez, and there were settlements on the long coastline which he might be able to "seize, surprise or take". Then a February rendezvous, well to westward of Acapulco, where he could lie in wait with all his force and take the galleon newly-laden with treasure.

Anson was well aware that this broad plan was, to say the least, uncertain of fulfilment. His ships, all desperately undermanned, were sorely in need of a dockyard refit; and there were a thousand chances and mishaps that might intervene before his little fleet forgathered off Acapulco. But his instinct was always to play for the highest stakes, and if the hand he held was not of the strongest he could trust in his own skill to play it to the best advantage. By the time *Centurion* and *Carmelo* dropped anchor in the bay of Juan Fernandez the dispositions for the first part of his plan were clear in his mind.

Tryal put to sea the morning after the Commodore's return. Her captain, Saunders, had orders to cruise off Valparaiso in search of prey. The prisoners from *Carmelo* and the half-dozen sick men still in need of nursing were put on board *Gloucester*, who was to proceed 1,800 miles to the northward and cruise on latitude 5° south, off the fortified port of Paita, where the rest of the squadron would eventually join her. A few days later she too was gone from the bay. For *Centurion*'s company there was hard work to be done before they could sail. *Anna*'s ten small guns were swung on board *Carmelo* and mounted, powder and shot supplied, water-casks filled and stored in her hold, food for a long voyage packed and stowed, and quarters prepared for Saumarez and the three petty officers and sixteen hands who were to man the prize.

On September 18th *Centurion* and *Carmelo* sailed out of the bay, leaving astern of them the sheltered green nook which had been both refuge and home for more than three months.

4

"The assault will be led by Mr Brett," said the Commodore.

His glance passed round the six officers seated at the table in the stern cabin: Brett, Saunders, Saumarez, Dennis, Colonel Cracherode, and Hughes, who was Saunders's lieutenant. The rich pink light of sunset

119

flooded in through the cabin windows, making them all look like Indians and dyeing the Colonel's grey moustaches in clownish manner. It was November, the 12th of the month, and the swift nightfall of the tropics would soon quench that fantastic radiance. The coming night would be moonless and its pitch darkness good cover for a surprise attack on the Spanish town of Paita.

"You will please to study this plan of the town with care, gentlemen," Anson continued, spreading a paper on the table. "It was provided, with other information I shall give you, by one of the prisoners from the *Carmine*."

Nuestra Señora del Carmine was the most recent of the three prizes taken since leaving Juan Fernandez. It was in fact only nine hours ago that Peircy Brett had taken her, with a boarding-party brandishing cutlasses and finding no foes to strike at. For the terrified Spaniards, so far from offering resistance, had embarrassed Brett by their abject pleas for mercy in return for any help or information they could give. There were advantages, it appeared, in having a reputation for bloodthirstiness. He had gleaned two valuable pieces of news. *Carmine* had sailed from Paita the previous day in considerable trepidation; a merchant ship entering the port had told of being chased by a large enemy vessel with patched and dirty sails. This could only be *Gloucester*, whose absence from the rendezvous off Paita had caused Anson some concern, and it was a relief to know that Mitchell and his crew were still afloat and active. The second piece of information was of more urgent nature. On hearing that an enemy ship was in the vicinity, the Governor of Paita had begun arrangements for moving a considerable treasure, stored in the Customs House of the port, to the town of Piura fifty miles inland. Brett had taken the news to *Centurion* at once and the same evening the Commodore had called this council of war.

"The town square appears to be your best rallying-place, Mr Brett," he was saying now, concluding his demonstration of the plan of Paita. "You will have two pilots from the prizes, men who know the town, as your guides and in the dark of the middle watch you'll need them. I have told them that if they play us false not only will they be shot instantly but also the eighty-five prisoners I propose to land here will be taken to England instead."

"God help us in that case," muttered Saumarez.

Anson's eyes twinkled. "Amen to that, Mr Saumarez. But you realise, of course, that I shall set them ashore in any case. We've not enough water and provisions to support an extra eighty-five." He looked at the colonel of marines. "Your men, Colonel, will embark in the barge. I'll be obliged if you, personally, will see that their muskets aren't loaded until they're ashore. A shot fired accidentally would remove our advantage of surprise. They will of course assault the fort without delay."

"Very good, sir," growled the colonel doubtfully. "I'll do what I can. But thirteen marines against a company of Spanish infantry—"

"You'll have support, Colonel." Anson turned to his acting first lieutenant. "Take forty-five seamen, Mr Brett—that's all we can spare. Pick them yourself. Mr Hughes will command one of the pinnaces and Mr Dennis the other. Now, gentlemen, have you any comments?"

"Yes, sir," said Brett. "I'd like to ask Colonel Cracherode if I may borrow the marines' drums. You still have them, Colonel?"

"I've two drums," said Cracherode gloomily, "but not one damned drummer. The bloody scurvy took 'em."

"From what I've seen of the Dons, sir, the more noise we make the faster they'll run," Brett said.

Anson nodded, "Very well. Mr Saumarez, Mr Saunders—you know your part in this."

"Aye, sir," said Saunders. "At first light we send our boats in and burn all vessels lying at anchor under the guns of the fort."

"It being assumed," Anson added drily, "that the fort is in our hands." He stood up. "Then that is all, gentlemen."

121

He detained Brett as he moved to pass out of the cabin with the rest.

"Two more words with you, Mr Brett. There's one Spaniard I'd prefer not to run from your drums, and that's the Governor. If you can take him and bring him on board, do so. He and I can then talk business."

"Concerning the ransom to be paid for Paita?" said the lieutenant quickly.

"Just so. He shall buy it from me." Anson's brief smile faded and left him grave. "One thing more, Peircy. I don't doubt you'll take this place. Only a magician could keep five-score seamen together on the streets of an enemy town in pitch darkness, but do your best. Keep them from spirits if you can but at all costs keep them from women. You will tell them that I'll have any man guilty of rape flogged round the squadron, a hundred lashes alongside every ship."

And that meant death, thought Brett.

"Aye, sir," he said.

Out on deck the hands were making ready to hoist barge and pinnace outboard. Night had almost come and a fast-fading orange glow in the west made black silhouettes of the four other ships lying hove-to within hail. All four were prizes. Besides *Carmine* and Saumarez's *Carmelo*, there was *Teresa*—taken by *Centurion* a week ago—and the much larger vessel now commanded by Saunders and renamed *Tryal's Prize*. Brett recalled, with a twinge of melancholy, the day at the end of September when they had sighted *Tryal* escorting an armed merchantman three times her size, which she had taken with the firing of a single broadside. The sloop herself had been dismasted in a sudden gale and was leaking like a sieve. After consulting with Saunders, Anson had decided to remove *Tryal's* guns and stores into the captured *Arranzazu*, a fine ship, and scuttle the unrepairable sloop. So they had seen the last of the gallant little vessel that had endured so much in their company. And with the Commodore's last remarks in his mind he remembered the taking of the *Teresa*, and the sudden tightening of Anson's jaw when Dennis, who had boarded her, reported that there were three women on board. These were a Spanish lady of quality and her daughters, all (said Dennis) of great beauty. Anson had ordered them to be confined in their cabin behind locked doors, with Spanish officers on guard night and day; his men had not seen a woman for well over a year. Brett wondered whether the Commodore's flat refusal to entertain these ladies, even to see them, meant that he too had felt the involuntary stirring of desire at the news of their presence and could not trust his own restraint.

"Sir!" said a voice at his elbow, and he turned to see Midshipman Keppel and a corporal of marines.

"Corporal Thompson, sir, has reported to me with two drums," said Keppel.

"The drumsticks is secured to 'em, sir," added Thompson. "If required, I can give instruction in the drumbeats, seeing as how—"

"That won't be necessary, Corporal." Brett was staring at the midshipman. "What the devil have you got on your head, Mr Keppel?"

"It's a leather jockey-cap, sir, with the peak turned up," said Keppel with dignity. "The idea, sir, is to give my skull some protection from a downward sword-cut."

"Very well." Brett hid his grin. "Convey my thanks to your colonel, Corporal. Mr Keppel, get for'ard and tell Mr Tully I want all hands mustered here on the after-deck."

As the two departed a seaman trotted aft and struck four double strokes on the bell that hung below the poop-deck. Eight bells of the last dog-watch. Brett glanced across the darkening sea, flat calm but just beginning to ruffle with the slight offshore breeze of evening. His boats had a fifteen-mile pull before them to reach their objective and the crews must have time to rest on their oars periodically; he had a clear hour for preparation before they need start.

123

5

The loom of the land was felt rather than seen as the three boats crept towards it through the darkness. In the stern-sheets of the eighteen-oared barge, which was leading with the two pinnaces astern, Peircy Brett handed over the tiller to Midshipman Keppel and stood up to peer into the black obscurity. The only glimmer of light was away on his left front and high up; that was probably the fort, overlooking the houses of the town and the anchorage where the ships lay. Half-a-mile still to pull to the landing-jetty, which should be right ahead.

"Sir!" came a low-voiced call from the lookout in the bows. "Small craft at anchor, larboard bow. I can 'ear voices, sir!"

Before Brett had time to curse this piece of bad luck there was a screech from the nearest vessel followed instantly by a babel of shouting from boats closer inshore. A pistol flashed and banged and he could hear the splash of oars receding towards the town. The Spaniards must have posted guard-boats ready to alert the defences, anticipating just such an attack. There was nothing he could do about that except land his men as quickly as possible.

"Pull, lads!" he shouted. "Get more way on her!"

Astern of him Hughes and Dennis were echoing his shout. Brett balanced himself against the forward surge of the barge and stared vainly into the blackness for some hint of the jetty's whereabouts. Ashore a bell was ringing and there was a curious rising hum that must be the collective voices of frightened or excited townspeople. Where was this damned jetty? Likely enough they'd posted a guard on it, but his boats were too precious to risk by driving them straight for a rocky shore. A yellow flash like lightning, above on his larboard hand. Then, almost simultaneously, the bang of the cannon and the distant splash of falling shot. The fort was firing at an unseen target but they knew where he was. They had eight guns up there, 4-pounders and 6-pounders. The Spanish pilot huddled on the bottom-boards at his feet was muttering prayers. And there, fine on the starboard bow, came three red flashes and the reports of muskets.

"Steer for the flashes," he snapped at Keppel; and to the men at the oars, "Pull—pull! A dozen strokes and we're alongside."

Another musket banged, and another. Brett felt the wind of a ball on his cheek as he bent to pick up the cutlass he had stowed beneath the stern thwart.

"'Vast pulling!" yelled Keppel frantically. "Bows, there!"

The barge swerved and rasped violently along the timbers of the wooden jetty which had loomed up suddenly from the darkness, its planking level with Brett's shoulder. He dragged one of his two pistols from his belt, cocked it, and fired along the jetty shoreward before clambering on to it. No one to oppose him, and the diminishing thud of running footsteps. Two guns fired in quick succession from the fort but there was no sign of their shot. Already Cracherode, volleying oaths, was on the jetty and his thirteen marines scrambling up to join him, and as Keppel hauled their Spanish guide out of the barge the two pinnaces came scraping alongside. A receding sound like thunder indicated that the marines were moving at the double to take up position on the foreshore as he had ordered, and bare cutlasses clinked and rattled as the barge's crew swarmed on to the planking.

"Follow!"

Brett ran along the jetty with Keppel and the guide at his heels and the seamen clumping behind. A glimmer of white blobs ahead showed the line of marines; beyond them at a distance muskets flashed and cracked.

"One volley and reload," said Cracherode's voice. "Present—fire!"

Thirteen muskets firing simultaneously made a fine resounding crash. By the brief light of their jetting flames

Brett could see his men forming in two uneven ranks.

"Mr Keppel! Bring that guide to the fore."

Close above were the houses and narrow streets of the town. He could make them out because of the jigging lights, torches or lanterns, that moved rapidly but irregularly up the streets away from him; Paita's inhabitants were evacuating the town.

"Damn my guts!" Cracherode was raving. "Reload, I said, not drop the bloody musket!"

Here came Hughes and Dennis with their seamen.

"Drums here!" Brett shouted, and two men with drums slung to their shoulders stood forward. "Now, lads, it's quick march and yell like devils. Sound off, drums! Come on!"

He strode forward as he spoke and the last two words were drowned in a deafening cacophony of noise. It was incredible that stretched calfskin and two pairs of sticks could produce such an uproar and yet it was nearly drowned by the cheering, whooping and bellowing of the men behind him. Brett led the way at a fast pace with Keppel and the guide close to him.

"*Izquierda!*" screeched the guide, and they swung to the left into a narrow street, unpaved and apparently deserted.

That fitted with the Commodore's plan of Paita. This street should lead into the main square, where the Governor's house formed one side and the wall of the fort another. Brett's orders for the assault, given before his parties embarked, had made the Paita treasure the prime objective of Hughes and his men; Hughes had with him the other Spanish pilot and he was to locate the Customs House, confirm that the treasure was there, and post a strong guard before coming to the main square. Dennis had been given the task of securing the person of the Governor while Brett's men and the marines stormed the fort, but that had assumed that the attackers would land unobserved. Now, with the defence alerted too soon, he would need Dennis's men as well as his own seamen and

126

the marines, and then he would only have four dozen for the attack on the fort. The Spanish informer had said that Paita could add 300 men to the gunners and infantry of the garrison. And there had been time for the gunners to shift those seaward-pointing cannon so that they could fire into the square. He quickened his pace.

No light showed in any of the houses they were passing, but ahead at the end of the street there was a dull red glow and a flicker of shadows. That would be the main square. Had the Spaniards set fire to the houses there? Brett broke into a run, and the close-packed mass of men burst yelling from the narrow street into the open space of the plaza. As they did so the fire that had been smouldering in a corner of the square flared up—a man had thrown straw on it—and the leaping flames showed the façade of a big house with a vine-wreathed balcony running across it. Muskets flashed and spat from the balcony but Brett had no time to think of that. To his left, opposite the house, was the wall of the fort, darkly illuminated by the blazing fire, with vague shapes moving on its upper rim.

"Follow! Follow!" he roared above the tumult, and ran for the wall with a crowd of seamen screeching and waving cutlasses close behind.

No ditch on this side. Six or seven feet of masonry. In the square behind him he heard the crash of a volley—the marines were in action against those musketeers on the balcony.

"Give me a heave," he snapped at Keppel, who had arrived panting at his side.

Keppel gripped his thighs and lifted until he could get his elbows over the parapet. All along the wall as he landed awkwardly on its inner side seamen were pouring into the dark square of the fort, yelling like fiends and waving their weapons. Their shouts died away comically when, after charging aimlessly here and there, they discovered that there was no enemy to oppose them. The little red eyes of glowing slow-matches, in buckets beside the guns along the seaward ramparts, were the only signs of recent occupancy.

"Mr Keppel! Mr Tully! Man these ramparts—a man every four paces. You two men come with me."

Brett groped his way round the walls with two seamen following him, stumbling in turn over a pile of round-shot and a discarded rammer. He found stone steps going downwards and ending in an open door which gave on to the hillside outside the town, and stood in the doorway for a moment to get his breath and allow his blood to regain its normal rate of circulation. This was the sally-port, and by it the garrison of the fort had fled without waiting to fight. He could see the outline of the low hills behind Paita in black silhouette against a paling eastern sky—daybreak was at hand, and this mere hint of light made it possible to make out the tall shape of the church that stood solitary and aloof from the town in Spanish colonial fashion. The faint breeze bore a murmuration in which he thought he could detect the clatter of hooves as well as the sound of many footsteps and voices; the people of Paita, as well as its garrison, were taking refuge beyond the crest of the hills. Brett suddenly remembered the Governor and wondered whether he was among them.

But there was much to do and he set about doing it. The fort was searched to ensure that no Spaniard remained in it, slow-matches extinguished and ready-use cartouches of powder removed to the magazine, and the small ensign that Brett had brought with him was hoisted on the flagpole on the outer rampart. When the heavy oaken door below the inner wall was unbarred and he walked out into the square it was almost full daylight. The only signs of the skirmish were two dead men on the balcony of the Governor's house and a blanket-covered figure lying against a wall; Hughes had arrived with half his party and Cracherode was inspecting his rank of thirteen marines. Dennis came trotting across the square to report.

"It's small trouble you had with the fort, Mr Brett, seemingly," he said with a grin. "We've one seaman dead and another wounded and the town of Paita's all ours."

"The Governor?" Brett demanded.

Dennis's grin faded. "He's five miles off by this. Got away in his nightshirt. The girl he was in bed with got away too—not a stitch on her. The lads up there—" he jerked a thumb at the balcony—"were covering his retreat, and they'd horses waiting behind the house."

Before Brett could comment on this news Lieutenant Hughes arrived to report the treasure safely under guard. And then came Midshipman Keppel, his jockey-cap shorn of its peak by a musket bullet, reporting that the squadron was hull-up and making for Paita; and then Colonel Cracherode requesting orders. Peircy Brett was receiving a first insight into the burdens of a commander-in-chief. He would have given his share of the Paita treasure for an hour's relaxation, but there was to be no rest for him that day, or indeed for forty-eight hours to come.

There was the disposition of his small force against the counter-attack that might well come, the removal of the treasure into the fort for its better defence, a foraging party arranged for the victualling of his men. Cracherode and Hughes with a few trusty men were despatched to scour the town and bring in any inhabitants that might still be lurking in the houses. A few old people and invalids were gathered in and taken to the church, where they were settled with food and drink and such comforts as could be found; a dozen Negroes, slaves, were released from their prison and set to work carrying the chests of silver plate and coins to the fort. Brett himself got to know the dirty streets of Paita like the back of his hand as he sped up and down them supervising the carrying-out of his orders. It was a comfort that the place now contained no women and little in the way of spirits, though there was wine in plenty. Even so, he was surprised and relieved by the good behaviour of his men. One foraging party of seamen, discovering a store of women's clothing, dressed themselves in frills and fur-belows and were discovered by Brett dancing a hilarious fandango in a courtyard; but his sharp remonstration (rendered difficult by their irresistibly comical appearance) set them about their duty with undiminished good-humour.

Later there was the report to the Commodore, with its admission of failure to secure the person of the Governor. Anson made no reproach. At once he sent one of the Spanish prisoners to find the refugees in the hills, with a letter to the Governor requiring him to arrange a ransom for the town; otherwise Paita would be burnt. No reply was received that day, and night found the invading force standing by in readiness for an attack on their position. Brett had information, confirmed by a lookout posted on the church steeple, that the Spaniards had collected a small army which included 200 well-armed horsemen and were preparing to descend on the town. No attack came, and a second letter to the Governor in the same terms as the first again brought no reply. Anson prepared to fulfil his threat; and before doing so he fulfilled his promise to put ashore all his Spanish prisoners. They were escorted to the church on the hillside well beyond the reach of flames while Brett and his men placed pitch, tar and other combustibles in all the houses on the windward side of the town. Meanwhile the collected treasure was being taken on board the ships (Walter valued it at £30,000) and in addition, pigs and poultry, fruit and vegetables, were taken to supplement the Expedition's stores. The sack of Paita was complete.

Saunders's boats were at work in the harbourage below the spiked and dismantled guns of the fort. The smoke from five burning ships was already spreading seaward when Paita began to burn. Brett with his rearguard came down at the double-march to the foreshore above the jetty, where their boats awaited them, and the men were halted to form line and be numbered.

"Fifty-six counting the marines," reported Tully, the

boatswain. "We was fifty-eight, sir, and Rigby's dead an' buried. One seaman missing, sir."

"It's McCombie—he ain't here," shouted more than one voice.

"Holy saints—look yonder!" Dennis exclaimed, cutting short further discussion.

Out from under the black smoke-cloud that drifted across the town came a dense crowd of men, at least 300 (thought Brett) and half of them on horseback. Those horsemen could be on them in ten seconds. There was no time to reach the boats.

"Cutlasses, lads," he said. "Stand firm."

"Marines—face about!" rasped Cracherode.

The horde of Spaniards had halted in some disorder, brandishing swords and shouting what sounded like insults.

"Marines—present! Wait for my word. Marines—God damn my guts and liver!" finished the Colonel angrily. "What's become of the bastards?"

Nothing confronted the marines' muskets but the rolling wall of smoke. As one man the Spaniards had taken to their heels and vanished into it.

"Seamen into the boats," said Brett, smothering slightly hysterical laughter. "Cover our retreat, Colonel, if you please."

But there was no need for cover. The enemy did not emerge again from the smoke-cloud. Only when the boats had shoved off and Brett, in the stern-sheets of the rearmost boat, was watching the shore for signs of pursuit did a solitary figure come reeling and stumbling out of the smoke to hurl himself off the end of the jetty with a mighty splash.

"That's McCombie, sir," said Keppel beside him. "He can't swim."

Seaman McCombie had swallowed a good deal of sea-water by the time he was hauled in over the gunwale. His messmates emptied it out of him, sniffing and grinning broadly the while; a very strong odour of brandy

131

accompanied the process.

"McCombie's clothes were charred to cinders, sir," Brett told the Commodore an hour later, ending his report. "He was lying drunk in a hovel when the flames reached it."

"He was fortunate," said Anson. "And I am fortunate in my officers. You did well, Mr Brett. I know of no other instance in naval history of a landing-party sacking an enemy town with only one man killed and a single seaman drunk."

"Thank you, sir. But the credit for orderliness must be given to the men. There was never a finer set of hands than those you have under you now, sir," Brett went on impulsively. "They can think for themselves as well as fight. They're mightily changed from the rabble we sailed with seventeen months ago."

"Yes," agreed Anson thoughtfully.

"If only you had the other six hundred with you—the six hundred that died," said Brett, "by God, sir, you could sack Panama!"

The Commodore was silent for a moment. Then he spoke with sudden sternness. "Very well, Mr Brett. Go and take what rest you may. The squadron will sail at first light tomorrow."

Next day the Expedition began the first stage of its long voyage northward, to Acapulco.

•

FIVE

The Maroons of Tinian

1

In years to come, Admiral Sir Peircy Brett was to look back on the months from November 1741 to August 1742 as the most trying period of his long and adventurous life. Those months held no such perils as had beset the Expedition off Cape Horn, no venture like that at Paita where boldness and discipline could confidently be pitted against a superior foe. The burden Brett found hardest of all to bear was his conviction—and not his alone—that the Commodore was making a fatal mistake in sailing on northward from Paita.

Brett knew that Saunders and Mitchell and Saumarez shared his misgivings; he also knew that neither he nor they could express them to their commanding officer. He himself had conceived an unbounded admiration for Anson and his faith and loyalty were unswerving. But in this stubborn quest for the Acapulco galleon he saw a wild throw in which all the dice were weighted against Anson, who stood to lose all he had won. And he had won so much. With his battered and undermanned ships he had taken five valuable prizes (the fifth, *Solidad*, had been the largest of those in the Paita anchorage) and much treasure; deprived of all the troops intended for land operations, he had yet sacked a fortified town and carried off still more treasure. Add to this that he had brought fear and dismay to the whole Spanish-American coastline by his presence and had caused Admiral Pizarro to lose half his valuable squadron, and no man could say that the Commodore had not fulfilled his mission despite the severest of handicaps. It would be a crowning triumph if he succeeded in returning to England across the four oceans, a ten-month voyage at the least, with the most valuable treasure won by any captain since the days of Drake. There would be hazard enough even in setting forth to cross the Pacific from Paita with the ships in such poor shape. But Anson, it seemed, was resolved to pile hazard on hazard, to linger for half-a-year more off this inhospitable coast where every man's hand was against him and every harbour closed to his vessels.

If the Commodore was aware of his officers' doubts he did not show it. And at the outset there was a sign that his good fortune still held, for hardly had the smoke of burning Paita vanished astern when he was joined by *Gloucester*. Captain Mitchell had taken only two prizes in his two months of cruising, both small vessels which he had destroyed; both of them, however, had been carrying doubloons and silver which added nearly £19,000 to the Expedition's booty. Mitchell had been delayed by the increasing decrepitude of his ship, whose leaky hull necessitated continual manning of the pumps and so reduced the already meagre number of men available to handle her. Anson, with a fleet of seven ships now under his command and barely enough men to man the largest of them efficiently, decided to dispense with two of them, *Teresa* and the newly-captured *Solidad*, which had proved to be the slowest sailers. Such of their gear as could be used was distributed among the other ships, and they were burnt. *Centurion* and *Gloucester*, *Tryal's Prize* and *Carmelo* and *Carmine*, stood to the northward together and crossed the Equator on November 22nd.

Now the calms and humid heat of the Doldrums were with them, the sails slatting feebly against masts and shrouds until some wandering breeze filled the worn canvas and enabled them to creep onward across the glassy blue for a few minutes. Quibo island, where they put in to fill the water-casks, provided them also with turtle-meat and wood for the galley fires. New Year's Day 1742 found the squadron battling with violent storms that alternated with sudden brief calms, and the struggles with the gales showed Anson only too plainly the danger of trying to man five ships with a total force of 300 men. He would not reduce his ships any further for all that; five ships were required for the plan he had devised to catch the Acapulco galleon and five he would retain. In improving weather they sailed on, north-westerly now, to make their landfall of the Mexican coast in early February.

What Anson needed now was information. To obtain it he sent away his barge with Dennis in command to probe the inshore waters while the squadron lay out of sight of land below the horizon. It took a fortnight to discover and confirm, from startled Spanish fishermen, that the treasure galleon was to sail on her annual voyage to Manila from Acapulco on March 3rd. The Commodore lost no time in making his dispositions to capture her. By March 1st the five ships were ranged in a semicircle with a radius of 45 miles from the port of Acapulco, each ship 9 miles from her neighbour. *Carmelo* and *Carmine*, at the ends of the arc, could keep observation over a further 18 miles from their mastheads, so that no vessel could pass unseen across a line 72 miles long. The cutters from *Centurion* and *Gloucester* were to patrol just out of sight of the port to give early warning if the galleon left harbour. Every man was eager and alert. The treasure, a quarter of a million pounds or more as it was reported, was as good as in their hands.

March 3rd came and passed and there was no sign of the galleon. The waiting hunters kept their stations. On board *Centurion* and *Gloucester*, the two vessels big enough to lay alongside the galleon, the hands were exercised daily in small-arms shooting and close range gun-drill. Days lengthened into weeks and still their intended prey did not sail into the net they had spread for her. Nor, indeed, did any other ship. At the end of three weeks there was only one conclusion to be drawn: Dennis's shoreward excursion had given the alarm and all Spanish vessels had been immobilised in harbour until Anson's ships had departed.

And depart they must, or perish from thirst. They had been four months at sea since leaving Quibo Island and the water they had left to them, already green and full of living organisms, would last at most six days. Anson's only information about supplies of water in these seas was from the writings of the buccaneers, and he resolved to make westward along the coast to an inlet, called Chequetan by William Dampier, where there was said to be a lake. It was found, and the five ships with their disappointed crews crept in to drop anchor in a small and sheltered bay. But the lake proved brackish, and the spring of fresh water was half-a-mile inland from its head, making the filling and loading of water-casks a long and laborious business. While it was being done Anson made the decision which some at least among his officers considered he should have made six months earlier. He would turn his back on the South American coast and sail for England.

To sail across the Pacific, 10,000 miles of voyaging to the nearest friendly harbour, needed not only a good navigator but also a well-found ship with a full complement of seamen. The Commodore could provide the navigation but not the ship or the men. The best he could do was to reduce his heavy handicap as much as possible before he sailed, and he took drastic action. *Carmine*, *Carmelo*, and *Tryal's Prize* were gutted of their stores, run on to the Chequetan beach, and burnt, not without grumbling from the crew of the latter who maintained that she was the soundest ship of the five. *Centurion* and *Gloucester* could now be manned with some degree of efficiency, though at only a third of their proper strength, and with full water-casks and provisions for two months the two ships—no longer to be called a squadron—sailed from Chequetan and stood to the south-west to pick up the trade winds in latitude 12½° North. On May 6th they had their last sight of the mountains of Mexico astern. They were to see no other land for fifteen terrible weeks.

For no sooner had the blue horizon completed its level circle round them than an increasing doom crept steadily upon the two ships. Not, this time, the savage gales of the Horn but a sultry calm began it, if calm it could be called when the glassy Pacific rollers tossed them ceaselessly under the windless sky. Week after week it endured, while the long unprofitable days of sweltering in tropical heat, captives in that one spot of ocean though the homeward road lay open, spread a growing depression through the crews. Anson alone remained confident and patient, even when disaster struck *Gloucester* with the loss of her mainmast. The perpetual rolling had sprung the mast, and when the carpenters began to attempt repairs it was found to be so rotten and decayed that they had to cut it down to a stump on which to step the topmast. *Centurion* herself sprung her foremast, and a leak in her bows made incessant pumping necessary. After two years at sea, with only temporary repair of the damage caused by many storms, both ships were fast becoming frail and unseaworthy.

And then the scurvy struck. Once again the hammocks in the 'tween-decks (there was ample space between them now) began to fill with sick men. Once again those hammocks, with their dead sewn in them, began to appear on deck every morning, two or three and sometimes more, to be hove overboard with brief ceremony. It was seven weeks—with better fortune they could have reached Macao in the time—before they felt at last the breath of the trade-winds, and by then the disease had both ships firmly in its stranglehold. There were not enough able-bodied hands in *Centurion* to reef and steer and man halyards and braces, let alone tend the growing number of sick, and Ettrick the surgeon laboured night and day with Richard Walter in the stinking "hospital" where the schoolmaster Pascoe Thomas was among their patients. In *Gloucester* officers and men toiled together at the pumps without cessation.

Yet now the brisk north-easters were carrying them steadily westward day after day, and despite everything the knowledge that each sea-mile covered brought them nearer to England gave heart to the seamen. Even in the sick-bay those who were able to speak, and the few that had begun to recover, talked eagerly of the China Sea and the rounding of the Cape of Good Hope and sailing past Ushant into the Channel—they could be home, with luck, before spring of next year. As for the Commodore, his invariable impassivity hid the anxiety that his officers showed more openly. It was now July and provisions were running short, while the water ration had already been cut to two-thirds. It had become impossible to sail direct to Macao as he had intended; the Ladrone islands were the only watering-place on his course, and there—if he could reach them—he would have to call. And since the largest of the Ladrones, Guam Island, was in the hands of the Spaniards, he would have to steer clear of it at all costs.

There was worse to come than this. At the end of July the trades suddenly yielded to a contrary wind from the west against which they were forced to beat. *Gloucester*'s jury spars could not stand the strain and she carried away foretopmast and foreyard. *Centurion* took her in tow while makeshift spars were erected, a task that took ten days because of the few men able to work, and no sooner was it completed than a heavy storm dismasted her completely. With seven feet of water in her hold and only the stumps of masts remaining, *Gloucester* was merely a wreck, while her crew was almost non-existent. Of her whole ship's company only sixteen officers and hands and eleven small boys were able to stand; she had seventy men sick.

Two days later the Commodore stood with Mitchell, captain of the *Gloucester*, at the stern-rail of *Centurion*'s poop-deck. Both men were silent, both stared across the spreading waves of the ship's wake to where a column of black smoke slanted across the grey sky of early morning. At the foot of the column came a sudden red flash from which smoke-clouds billowed upwards.

"Magazine," said Mitchell; he cleared his throat noisily. "She's gone."

He turned and went down to his cabin. Anson remained immobile, gazing at the receding smudge of smoke without seeing it. His inner vision was fixed on a darker cloud. *Centurion* was alone. All the officers and men of an Expedition that had sailed two thousand strong were on board—two hundred, of whom seventy-one were able to stand. It had proved impossible to transfer the few remaining water-casks from *Gloucester*'s flooded hold and he had only enough water left for a few days on half ration. By his last reckoning the ship was some 300 miles east of the Ladrones but in the empty wastes of the Pacific it would be easy to miss the islands altogether. If he passed them, if they were left to windward, he could never retrieve the mistake; and the next land was 1,888 miles beyond. They would be dead, every man, of thirst and scurvy long before they could reach it. He had to find the islands.

2

The ship that heaved herself sluggishly forward over the long Pacific swell wore Spanish colours aft and a red flag at her foretopmast head. The guns on her upper deck were loaded and run out but they could hardly be said to be manned; the two or three men at each gun lay or squatted on the deck, conserving their feeble strength for the moment of action. The light breeze that wafted her slowly towards the low green hump that broke the blue of the horizon was the gentlest of airs, yet there were two quartermasters to handle the wheel, one of them a big man in a ragged red coat and the other a man of middle size whose pale blue eyes gleamed above a grey stubble of beard.

"Meet her as the bows swing, Corporal," croaked Commodore Anson.

"Yessir," said Corporal Thompson.

The Commodore tried to moisten his cracked lips. "You should say 'Aye, sir,' " he said hoarsely.

"Yessir—I mean aye, sir," said the corporal of marines.

Up on the wooden planking of the foretop a man in soiled shirt and breeches, gaunt and unshaven, linked an arm round the foretopmast stay and steadied his glass on the island they were approaching. *Centurion* had few men left capable of going aloft and Lieutenant Peircy Brett was one of them. There were three islands in sight from the masthead but two of them were distant streaks on either bow; the middle island for which the ship was making was certainly one of the Ladrones, and it was not large enough, Brett knew, to be Spanish-occupied Guam. There could well be Spaniards on it, all the same, and enemy ships in an anchorage, ready to fall on an easy prey. Anson had done what he could to disarm early suspicion by hoisting Spanish colours and flying the red flag which was customary, but it was a safe landing rather than an escape to sea that was needed, and desperately needed, now.

A speck danced in the hazy circle of Brett's glass. He made certain of it, then hailed the deck as loudly as his dry throat would allow.

"Boat heading to meet us, sir—a proa."

The native boat with its outrigger and lateen sail could mean that the island was inhabited only by savages, Indians. *Centurion* held on her slow way and the boat came rapidly closer. With the glass, Brett could make out five men in her, though he could only guess at their colour and clothing. Beyond, the island began to reveal tree-clad slopes with wide green spaces under them and oddly-shaped masses of rock rising above. There was a shed or hut near the shore—

140

"Mr Brett!" It was the Commodore hailing him. "Come down, if you please."

"Aye, sir."

He clambered down the ratlines, conscious of the physical weakness that made his fingers tremble as they grasped each rope-rung, and went aft at a stumbling trot. Hands were casting loose the lashings of cutter and pinnace, and Saumarez, his sun-blistered face almost hidden by a spiky black beard, was receiving Anson's orders.

"I want the men from that proa before she takes fright and makes off, as she will do if I close her in this ship." The Commodore turned to his second lieutenant. "You'll take the pinnace, Mr Brett, and Mr Saumarez the cutter. The cutter will hold on for the island to seek anchorage and landing-place, the pinnace will bring the proa men on board."

It was as well that the proa had not been allowed to come too close to *Centurion*. As it was, only the threat of the muskets in the pinnace stopped her from putting about before she could be seized. Four of her occupants were Indians but the fifth was a Spaniard who had been deceived by *Centurion*'s false colours. He was squat and ugly, but an angel could not have brought more welcome tidings than the information he provided when Anson questioned him. The island they were approaching was called Tinian and it was uninhabited. He himself was a sergeant sent from distant Guam with twenty-two Indians to bring back a cargo of jerked beef; for the colony and garrison of Guam used Tinian as a kind of supply store, and cattle and poultry roamed wild on the island, which was also exceptionally rich in fruit of all kinds. He had landed a few days ago, and his fifteen-ton barque was at anchor close inshore with the rest of his Indian crew on board. He would not be expected back in Guam, added the sergeant, for a month or more.

So, piloted by Saumarez in the cutter, *Centurion* crept cautiously in to a haven even more welcome than that of

Juan Fernandez nearly a year and three months ago. It was mid-afternoon when she let go her anchor in twenty-two fathoms, a scant half-mile from the shore where the long rollers broke against terraces of pink and grey coral. Above the shore they could see cattle grazing on meadow-like pastures, and the sparkle of clear streams, and trees hung with yellow fruit, a vision of paradise to parched and weary men. But they were not to attain it that day. Their one remaining link with home, the ship, took priority over all other needs and she had to be made safe in an anchorage that was far from perfect, being exposed to south and east and having poor holding-ground in the sharp coral. Saumarez with the strongest men had been sent to seize and occupy the barque. It took the remainder in *Centurion* five hours to furl the sails, a task which had been accomplished in five-and-a-half minutes by Peircy Brett's watch while the ship was at Madeira; and by the time all the other work of making snug had been done every man was exhausted and there were some who dropped to the deck-planking and slept where they lay.

The morning of August 28th saw the beginning of the landing of the sick men. Brett, who had landed first with an armed party in case the Spaniard's report had been false, shouldered into the surf to begin the carrying and found himself helping the Commodore to haul the boat's bows up the shingle.

"The hut we saw is a big store-house, sir," he shouted above the roar of the breaking waves. "Twenty paces by twelve and a sound roof. My lads are clearing it now."

"Excellent." Anson steadied himself with a hand on the gunwale as the surf boiled round his thighs. "We'll carry straight to it. You and I are of a size, Mr Brett, so we'll work together as we did at Fernandez. Ready? Lift!"

The first limp figure to be carried ashore was the schoolmaster. Pascoe Thomas was too weak to raise a hand but he could still talk.

"Limes—the juice of limes," he babbled as they toiled

142

with him up the terraces of coral. "They grow here. Limes, sir—limes, Mr Brett. Promise me I'll have limes. The juice of limes can save me and nothing else will."

Brett gasped out the required promise and Thomas relapsed into apparent insensibility. They got him into the big store-hut, just cleared of the hides it had contained, and left 'him to the care of Ettrick, who had landed from the second boat. Pairs of seamen were struggling up from the beach with their invalid burdens as Anson and Brett walked down.

"The juice of limes," Anson repeated meditatively. "Was this a delirium, Mr Brett, or matter more weighty?"

"There could be weight to it, sir." Brett told briefly of the discussion between Thomas and the chaplain on Juan Fernandez. "The surgeon maintains that acid juices can only be harmful to the stomach," he added.

"And your own opinion?"

"I'm no physician, sir," said Brett, "but I had it in mind to suggest that a store of fruits should be taken with us when we left Fernandez. It's on my conscience that I neglected to make that suggestion, sir."

Anson was frowning thoughtfully as he stepped down the coral foreshore. "The fruit would quickly rot," he said. "It must be pressed and put in cask. We'll try this, Peircy, when we sail from Tinian. And I will overrule Ettrick and give orders for all sick men to be given lime-juice henceforth." He halted at the edge of the surf to let two grunting seamen pass with their load. "I've put my share of the Paita treasure into the lower-deck pool, as you know. I'd give every penny of prize-money if I could save the men I have left."

He spoke the last words with unusual feeling. Was he, Brett wondered, thinking of the men as human beings, or merely as necessities for the working of his ship? A captain must of course put his ship before all else—

"Look sharp there, Mr Brett!" said the Commodore, leaning into the green curve of a breaking wave.

Brett splashed hastily after him to the side of the boat.

143

"Take hold—lift!"

They began the second journey of a score and more.

There were 128 sick men to be got up on to *Centurion*'s deck, lowered into boats, and carried up from the beach. It took two days to complete the task with every available officer and man working at it, and only then could they begin to establish themselves for a stay that seemed likely to be at least as long as their time on Juan Fernadez. In the fair weather that prevailed the island was a delectable place. The Spanish sergeant, with the casual philosophy of his race accepting his new masters easily, showed them how to catch and butcher the cattle; the Indians from the barque led them to the most fruitful groves. A diet of fresh food swiftly restored the health and strength of those who were free from scurvy, and although twenty-one of the sick men died in the first two days the death-rate thereafter fell with such rapidity that at the end of two weeks only six men more had died. Among these was Anson's servant, Ham. The Negro had shown a resistance to hardship and privation that put many a white man to shame; but it was the nature of the disease to strike at weak and strong alike, and always with the fiercest stroke for the strong. Ham sickened and died within three days, and this despite the administering of lime-juice which seemed to have had such a remarkable effect on the other invalids. The Commodore had devised a press for the limes that grew in profusion above the foreshore, turning a deaf ear to Ettrick's protests, and the results (except in the case of Ham) had justified the experiment. Pascoe Thomas, who had made a swift recovery, now found a ready convert in Walter the chaplain and the two of them patrolled the hospital hut with beakers of fruit-juice while the disapproving surgeon relieved his feelings by blood-letting according to the best professional doctrine.

Meanwhile every fit man was hard at work on *Centurion*. There could be no lotus-eating on Tinian; as on Juan Fernandez, the threat of an enemy warship appearing suddenly off the island was ever present. And—as on Juan Fernandez—the first task was to cleanse the ship of the filth and stench in her 'tween-decks. When that was done the leak that caused her pumps to be manned continuously during the week before Tinian was sighted had to be found and dealt with. This was located close to her stem, and since she could not be hove-down anywhere on that coral shore her bows had to be raised out of the water. It was a week's task to shift the 130 barrels of gunpowder from the forepeak, haul all the for'ard guns aft, and strip the sheathing on both sides of the cutwater, and when at last the laborious work of caulking and re-sheathing was done and the ship brought to an even keel again there was still a considerable leakage. The stem itself was cranky, and nothing could be done about that until she could be got out of the water.

Centurion was posing another problem—that of her poor anchorage. The Commodore, with his first and second lieutenants and Captain Mitchell, was debating this problem on a brilliant afternoon of mid-September. The four men were sitting together in the shade of a massive buttress of pink coral that jutted from the foreshore, with the rhythmical thunder of the Pacific surf in their ears. Out across the dazzling blue *Centurion* rose and fell on the waves, her rigging dotted with the tiny figures of the boatswain's party who were overhauling stays and shrouds.

"New moon's on the eighteenth," Mitchell was saying, his deep-sunk eyes narrowed to stare at the ship. "That's when we can expect a gale or two."

"And a southerly would catch her with her breeches down," added Saumarez. "I don't trust those cables."

"I'll have the main and fore yards off her," Anson said. "We have enough hands to do it, and it would help her to ride out a gale."

His speech, Brett noticed, was unusually slow and a trifle indistinct. The Commodore had been deeply affected, he knew, by the death of his servant three days

145

ago; perhaps this had something to do with it.

"We've the small bower out," said Saumarez, "and the best bower. Even on a coral bottom they should hold her. But the cables, sir—they're bound to chafe on the coral." He patted the rock at his side. "It's like a million penknives set on edge."

"Arm the cables, then," said Anson; he seemed to get the words out with an effort. "Use chain on the sections next to the anchors." He rose slowly to his feet. "See to that now, Mr Saumarez. Captain Mitchell, you'll oblige me by supervising the operation."

"Aye, sir."

As the two moved away the Commodore stumbled and would have fallen but for Brett's quick support, and he kept a hand on the lieutenant's arm while they mounted to the grassy slope above the foreshore. As soon as they reached it Anson sank down on the grass.

"I shall remain here," he announced calmly, "while you fetch a couple of strong seamen, Mr Brett. Perhaps you had better bring Mr Ettrick also."

"You're ill, sir!" Brett exclaimed. "Is it—?"

"I fear so." Anson drew back his coat-sleeve. "I have tried to ignore these but to no avail."

His forearm was covered with dark-purple blotches. Brett, shocked and stammering his concern, was cut short abruptly.

"I'll have a tent rigged by the grove of limes yonder. Captain Mitchell will command until I'm recovered. Tell Ettrick I am not to be bled. And—carry on, Mr Brett, and look lively."

The last words were spoken with a faint smile but the glance of the pale-blue eyes was imperative. Brett turned and ran across the grass towards the hospital hut.

Twenty-four hours later the Commodore lay in his improvised tent too weak to lift his head, helpless in the grip of scurvy.

3

"You're stepping it like a March lamb this morning, sir," said Vokes. "Ain't he now, Purvis?"

"A marked improvement, sir, indeed," said Purvis.

He was a younger man than Vokes though equally tall, and his tenor voice sounded oddly refined in contrast with Vokes's deep country burr. There was more contrast still between the mahogany skins of the two seamen and the sickly pallor of the man who walked between them, supporting himself with his arms across their shoulders. Whether or not because of Pascoe Thomas's fruit-juice treatment, the Commodore was making a notably quick recovery from his attack of scurvy, so much so that yesterday—disregarding Ettrick's protests—he had sent orders to Saumarez for two seamen of equal height to come to his tent and assist in getting him back on his feet. On their first essay at this exercise, pacing slowly back and forth on the grassy terrace above the shore, Vokes and Purvis had been so embarrassed by close contact with their commander-in-chief that they had been practically tongue-tied. Anson, his hard shell of reserve broken by illness, had found himself making conversation to set them at their ease and avoid the long silences broken only by his own gasps and grunts. In this he had succeeded so well that on this second morning the seamen were talking naturally, albeit with due respect.

"If I'm improving," he said now to keep the conversation going, "it is more than can be said for the weather."

"Right you are, sir," Vokes said, glancing out to sea. "It's dark, like. Might be the Horn, almost.—Ready to go about, sir?"

The three shuffled round and began to move back towards the tent. Down on their right the breakers roared sullenly on the coral beach, and a sea the colour of purple grapes heaved restlessly beneath the overcast sky. There was not a breath of wind, yet *Centurion* half-a-mile off shore was soaring and swooping at her anchors as the huge oily waves passed under her.

"Typhoon," Purvis said suddenly. "I beg your pardon, sir, but I was trying to remember the name of a storm that occurs in these waters."

"You've sailed in this region before?" Anson asked with unfeigned interest.

Purvis's reply had an undertone of bitterness. "No, sir. This is my first voyage—I was pressed at Portsmouth."

Anson was silent for a moment, hobbling on his shaky legs while he clung to his supporters. He was conscious of curiosity. What effect had this landsman's first voyage—and such a voyage!—had upon him?

"You were in a tavern, I suppose, when the press-gang caught you," he said.

"I was in a brothel, sir," said Purvis without any expression in his voice; he paused while they took three steps and then went on in the same tone. "It's two years ago and it seems like twenty. I was usher in a school at Cosham. There was a girl—well, she threw me over for another man. I went into Portsmouth. *Injuriarum remedium est oblivio*, I thought. It was a petty officer's cudgel that brought oblivion—until I was being hauled on board *Centurion*. I've learned a great deal since then, sir."

"You've learned as how you wasn't a man before, me lad," said Vokes, plainly impatient to have his share of the Commodore's attention. "Now me, sir, I was took out of Portsmouth gaol to be made a seaman of, and I ain't regretted it only once or twice, sir."

The impulse to check this unprecedented gossiping with a reprimand sharply uttered was strong in Anson. What concern had he with the former lives of these men, or their feelings? His interest should begin and end with their capacity as hands—the human mechanism for hauling on ropes and firing guns. Perhaps it was the lingering debility of his illness that caused him to give way to Vokes's obvious eagerness to talk.

"And how came you in Portsmouth gaol?" he asked.

"Sheep-stealing, sir," said Vokes, not without pride.

148

"Waiting transportation, I was.—Go about, sir? Round she comes."

Transportation to the American colonies, thought Anson as they shuffled round to recommence their walk, was bad enough, but some of the convicts he had seen in Carolina led a life far less hard than that of a seaman on *Centurion*'s lower deck.

"Now there's a trade," Vokes went on, making the most of his chance to talk, "I mean sheep-stealing, sir, as takes a deal of craft and cunning. Not but what a seaman's trade don't take craft and cunning too—more, come to think on it. Nay, I'll say this. There's more for a man in being a seaman than what there is in being a sheep-stealer."

"You are content, then, with your present trade?" Anson asked.

They advanced four slow paces while Vokes thought that over.

"Content, sir?" he said at last heavily. "If so be's you mean am I happy, sir, I reckon that's what I am. At this present time, like. It took two year to get me that way, it being as you might say a proper tussle for a pressed landsman to win any happiness, matters being arranged so as he can't use his wits and anyways his wits is scared out of him—"

"What Vokes is trying to say," Purvis cut in with sudden impatience, "is that we're proud to call ourselves seamen of the King's Navy and ashamed of the way that was used to make us so. It was a bad way and a wasteful way. I'm aware the officers aren't to blame. You yourself—"

"Avast there, Purvy!" interjected Vokes, with an apprehensive side-glance at the Commodore.

"You yourself, sir," Purvis hurried on without heeding him, "have to suffer the grievous negligence of the naval authorities, fobbing you off with rotten ships and useless troops for a mission like this. Reform is what is needed, reform at the top, by a man like yourself who knows—"

"*Still!*" rasped the Commodore, summoning all his feeble strength and putting it into his voice.

149

The three came to a halt, in silence. Anson, inwardly cursing his folly, spent a second or two considering what action to take. The young fool Purvis had laid himself open to a charge of mutiny by his words, but he, Anson, had invited plain speaking from the men and was himself partly to blame.

"I shall forget what you have just said, Purvis," he announced coldly. "But if I find you speaking in that manner again, on the lower deck or elsewhere, I'll have you flogged. And it'll be a flogging for both of you if any word of this conversation is mentioned to your messmates. You understand?"

"Aye, sir," they said together.

"Help me to my tent," snapped Anson

An hour later, when Ettrick had attended to him and departed, he lay on his palliasse marvelling at his own injudicious behaviour. It was the essence of command to maintain the strict aloofness that symbolised his unquestionable superiority to his men. He had stupidly relaxed that rule—and see what had happened. It would not happen again. Strength was fast coming back to his legs and tomorrow he would take his walk with the aid of a staff, which Mitchell, when he came to make his evening report, should be told to provide.

Captain Mitchell's report was not an encouraging one. The task of getting the filled water-casks on board *Centurion* had not been completed because of the increasingly heavy swell, which prevented the laden boats from being launched from the beach. There was still no wind, but so huge were the waves that communication with the ship was virtually impossible. Saumarez and Brett were on board with a stowing party and so was Cracherode and his thirteen marines; they would have to remain there until the swell moderated. Anson received this news with his usual imperturbability and did not forget to ask Mitchell, as he departed, to detail a seaman with a sharp knife to cut him a stout staff; but this interruption of his programme, and the threat of bad weather suggested by the abnormal swell, were disappointing. They had been four weeks on Tinian now and he had hoped to sail within the next few days. Yet, as he tried to compose himself for sleep, it was not the problem of *Centurion*'s sailing that occupied his restless mind but the words of the seaman Purvis. He had told Purvis that he would forget what he had said; but to his annoyance he found that he could not.

Next day at noon the wind came. Anson's tent and the store-house (where a mere half-a-dozen sick lay now) had full shelter from the wooded bluffs above, and only an occasional powerful gust drove at them round the corner of the hills, but out to sea there was furious turmoil. The swift tidal current that ran at intervals between Tinian and the neighbouring islands had already caused some anxiety on account of the overfalls it created. Now the gale was meeting the current head-on, and wind met wave in a battle of giants that took no account of the vessel in their midst. *Centurion* had little or no lee from the storm and she was tossed skyward and lost to sight in the troughs as the black sea-mountains marched smoking upon her. Miraculously her anchors were holding; but the high-pitched howl of the gale tearing through the volcanic outcrops above the landing-place rose higher hour by hour.

At mid-afternoon the Commodore was huddled in the shelter of the coral buttress above the shore where he had sat with his officers nearly three weeks earlier. Aided by his stout stick and by Saunders and Mitchell, who crouched beside him, he had hobbled there to watch over his ship though he could do nothing for her. The hundred-odd men who had been left ashore were watching too from the shelter of rock or bush. Mitchell voiced the anxieties of them all.

"God send those cables hold!" he said, his mouth close to Anson's ear to make himself heard above the tumult. "If they don't, she's lost."

Anson said nothing. He saw, perhaps more clearly than

151

Mitchell, the fate that awaited them if *Centurion* was swept from her anchorage. Her mainyards had been sent down and the few on board could hardly hope to rig them again. In utter helplessness she would be driven far to leeward, a hundred miles or a thousand according to how long the storm persisted, and even if she survived her weak crew would in all probability be unable to bring her back to Tinian. He and his men would be marooned on this Pacific island, two thousand miles from the nearest friendly port. Eventual discovery by the Spaniards from Guam, imprisonment or slavery or even death if they tried to make a fight of it—

But *Centurion* was still fighting for her own life. With his glass, when the huge waves and racing spindrift allowed him to see her, he could make out movement on her deck. Some resolute souls were trying to make fast the longboat, which was moored to the ship's stern. Saunders, who had his own glass to his eye, gave a sudden cry and Anson winced as if he had been hit. The longboat had been picked up on the crest of a mighty wave and hurled at *Centurion*'s high stern, smashing its galleries. Splintered woodwork could momentarily be seen flying horizontally on the resistless blast. The longboat had gone, cutter and pinnaces were drawn up on the beach below, and those on board *Centurion* could neither tow nor abandon her.

The storm—typhoon, if that was what it was—showed no sign of abating as afternoon darkened towards evening. The watchers on shore saw the flash of a gun and knew that Saumarez was signalling some dire emergency. *Centurion*'s violent tossing altered its nature and her yardless masts came in line.

"Best bower's gone!" shouted Mitchell. "Small bower must have parted earlier—she's going!"

The ship plunged and rose and already she was well to leeward of her former position. As if in triumph, the eldritch screeching of the gale rose yet higher among the crags behind the shore and across the chaos of the sea the driven screen of spume and spray thickened to hide her.

152

A brief clearance showed her imperfectly, the small dark ghost of a ship tossed among ferocious waves. Then she was gone, lost in the dark spaces of the Pacific.

The Commodore hauled himself to his feet with the aid of his staff and a hand on the coral rock.

"Post lookouts on the hilltop and relieve them every two hours, Captain Mitchell, if you please." His voice had regained its old incisiveness. "Captain Saunders, I shall be glad of your assistance as far as my tent."

Ettrick was waiting in the lee of the swaying tent. Anson waved away his inquiries and proffered medicines impatiently and dismissed both his helpers; from now on he must stand on his own feet, relying on the force of his will to keep him there. In this emergency he must be seen by his men to be a strong and confident leader, not the shambling cripple he had been these last three weeks. He crawled unaided on to his palliasse and lay there beneath the flapping canvas, calmly foreseeing and facing the immediate future.

The odds against their ever seeing *Centurion* again were at least a hundred to one. The continuation of his voyage—for he was already resolved to continue it—had to be made without her. The means for that were to hand, and inadequate though they were he would use them. He could visualise his course on the crude chart he possessed, nor' westerly to reach the 22nd parallel and then west in that latitude to clear the southern tip of Formosa and so to the mouth of the Canton river, where he would find safe haven and help for the onward journey in the Portuguese port of Macao. Two thousand miles; a little more or a little less. Even with favouring winds the voyage would take three weeks or a month, and a typhoon like the storm that was blowing now would mean an end to the venture once and for all. For Anson proposed to use the little fifteen-ton barque in which the Spanish sergeant had come from Guam.

"Five days have passed since Centurion went adrift," said Anson; his voice was raised to reach the outermost fringe of the crowd of men before him. "We can no longer hope for her return."

He paused to let that sink in, his keen glance passing across the brown faces. They were a ragged throng enough, and the group of officers standing to one side were little better; Dennis's red hair flowed in ringlets down his breast from under a travesty of a hat, Baird who had been Gloucester's first lieutenant wore a shirt made of broad leaves, presumably to hide some serious gap in his breeches. The tall ruffian with a fuzz of black beard and a torn shirt must be Midshipman the Honourable Augustus Van Keppel. All told, there were 113 men marooned on Tinian, including himself.

"We shall begin the enlargement of the barque at once," he went on. "By good fortune all our carpenters are here and I have conferred with them. They agree that if we lengthen her by twelve feet she will be near forty tons when she's planked and decked. Every man who hears me now will do his share of the work and I shall expect no more from any man than I can perform myself—if there's one among you that can handle an axe better than I can I'll be surprised."

There were a few grins and chuckles at that. When they had been mustered in this grassy hollow the men had seemed dull and dispirited; and with more reasons than one to be so, Anson reflected. The lost vessel had borne away with her what amounted to a small fortune for every man here, so that if ever they returned to England it would not be as the affluent heroes they had pictured but as penniless refugees. He remembered the one slim chance he had considered possible and decided to raise their spirits with it.

"When the barque is ready for sea we shall sail for Macao," he told them, "and it's not impossible that we shall find *Centurion* there. She was blown to the westward, maybe for many hundreds of miles, and good seamen though they are on board they're too few to sail her back against the Trades. But Macao lies to westward, and if Mr Saumarez finds he's half-way there I don't doubt he'll sail on to get provisions and water for his crew."

That brought a stir of excited movement and a buzz of muttered comment. Anson arrested it with a hand upraised.

"Very well. We shall work watch and watch. Officers, muster your parties. Lookouts to your stations. Carry on."

It was September 27th when work on the barque began, and on that day and succeeding days the swing of the Commodore's axe set the example of steady work which his men faithfully imitated. Anson had not yet recovered his full strength after the bout of scurvy, but the practised skill that laid blade to mark compensated for bodily weakness; tree-felling in the woods of Colwich had always been a favourite exercise of his since childhood. Coconut palms and other trees of a girth suitable for planking fell and were measured, trimmed, and sawn, while parties toiled at the other tasks according to the plan worked out with Saunders and Mitchell before he addressed the men.

No one knew better than Anson the magnitude of the task they were undertaking. In a naval dockyard, with dry dock and shipbuilding resources to hand, the lengthening of a small ship would have presented few problems, but on Tinian they had no dock and few tools. Burton the smith had forge and hammer on shore but not bellows; cowhide and a musket-barrel were used to make the bellows and the forging of the ironwork went ahead. Shifts of the strongest men laboured with pick and spade to excavate a dry dock well above high-water mark. *Centurion* had borne away all the spare blocks and cordage that could have been used for hauling the barque up to the dock, so rollers made from the coconut-palms would have to be used, with slots in either end to take the levers by which she would be brought up inch by inch to the high-and-dry bed where she could be sawn in half. The dozen or so men who were still weak after recovering from scurvy worked at the gathering and pressing of limes and sour oranges. In weather that had remained fair and cool ever since the storm had blown itself out on its third day, the work progressed amain; but in the first days of October, when it began to be possible to assess the rate of progress, the Commodore could fix their sailing date no earlier than November 5th.

Anson, toiling alongside his men with axe and adze, came to know more about them in those weeks than he had learned in twenty-four months of voyaging. Working with Corporal Thompson of the marines and Tully the boatswain one day, with Vokes and Midshipman Keppel another, he warmed to their acceptance of himself as a comrade rather than a commander. His physical strength had returned in full, the loss of the men in *Centurion* (in particular Peircy Brett whom he had come to regard as a friend) had dulled its first keen impact, and he would have been happy but for the frustration of an increasing purpose.

It was a purpose hardly realised, not yet completely formulated. Perhaps it had been at the back of his mind for some time, moving stealthily forward into a vague beginning of thought during his illness. Anson could trace its origins in past incidents and past words, from Purvis's ill-advised utterance to phrases used by Brett and Saunders and—so long ago that it seemed in another life—to things that Lord Hardwicke and his daughter had said when he had visited the house in Downing Street. The idea had grown from a thing rejected to an urgent purpose without conscious encouragement on his part, and only when the means of fulfilling it were rudely torn from him had Anson understood how important it had become to him. For above all it demanded his return to England triumphant, successful, a hero deserving of high honours and a place of authority in the State. Now the chance was gone, perhaps for ever. If he returned it

156

would be as a failure who had lost all his ships and the whole of the vast treasure he had taken from the Spaniards, his new ambitions too ridiculous to be considered. His old reliance on his grand ally Fortune had gone with his old arrogant confidence in himself. It was a new George Anson that had crawled feebly out of his tent when the scurvy had run its course.

This disappointment did not lose its edge but rather increased in sharpness. Now that the opportunity had been removed, the schemes and projects that could have developed from it proliferated in Anson's mind in spite of all his efforts to forget them, and the further the work on the barque progressed the more poignant his regret became. None of the men who worked with him would have suspected this, however. The Commodore's angular face, rendered thin by illness and burned red-brown by the sun, showed only an imperturbable calm which remained unchanged through all the minor mishaps and checks of the boat-building.

And steadily the preparations went on. Ten days after the beginning of the work the ribs and keelson for the new middle section were shaped and ready, and the rollers were laid and the barque hauled up with great labour to the sandy hollow that was to serve as a dock. On October 8th, two days later, she was sawn in half and the two ends drawn apart to the exact distance for the new timbers; and that same night a fierce thunderstorm broke for the first time the continued good weather. All this time the lookouts had kept continuous watch from the hilltop that commanded a wide arc of ocean. And on October 11th, when they had kept that watch for nineteen days, came the event that changed the future of every man on Tinian.

It was mid-afternoon of a clear cool day and the ship-building party was hard at work, Anson among them. The Commodore was using an axe to trim one of the ribs when a frantic yell from the slopes above the "dock" made everyone look up. A man was racing down

157

the hillside waving his arms and shouting, and the two words of his shout made every man about the barque throw down his tool and raise his voice like a multipicity of echoes.

"The ship—the ship!"

Walter the chaplain was on his knees close to Anson, working with hammer and chisel at the keelson joint. His quick upward glance showed him something he was never to forget: for the first and only time in two years of repeated disaster and recovery he saw the Commodore overcome by emotion. Anson let fall his axe and hid his face in the bend of his forearm. So he stood, with lowered head, for a few seconds. Then he turned and ran with the rest of the excited men to the bluff farther along the shore whence the ocean to south and east could be viewed.

Afterwards he was to wonder a little at the certainty he had felt, in common with everyone else by the barque, that the sail that had been sighted was indeed *Centurion* and not some enemy vessel. But the lookouts had made certain of her before sending down the news; a three-masted ship with no mainyard crossed and one patched and dirty square of canvas on the fore could only be their own missing vessel returned. And so it proved. It was five o'clock before *Centurion*, making very slow progress, was in the offing and near enough for a boat to be sent off to her with water and fresh food and eighteen hands to assist her exhausted crew, and the afternoon of the next day when she at last cast anchor and Saumarez came ashore to report his adventures. The gale had driven them southward for five days; when the weather had at last abated they had little or no idea of their position except that they must be some hundreds of miles south of Tinian. All attempts to hoist the mainyard had failed, a man being killed by the falling yard during one attempt, but in the end they had managed to get a yard rigged on the foremast and sail hoisted on it. Increasingly hampered by shortage of food and water, Saumarez and Brett between them had plotted and sailed their dubious northward course for fourteen days and their good seamanship had brought the landfall they had hoped for.

There were celebrations; seamen deprived of their rum-ration for nearly three weeks had naturally to be given just compensation in kind, even though the work of filling *Centurion*'s water-casks, interrupted when she went adrift, was at once resumed on Anson's orders. Two seamen, Cross and Stevens, lost their lives as the result of this bounty, for in a drunken fight they dislodged a row of filled casks they had placed insecurely on the hillside and were crushed to death in the ensuing avalanche of casks. Apart from this untoward incident the work of preparing the returned *Centurion* for the onward voyage went on swiftly. Fresh fruit, coconuts, and pressed lime-juice were taken on board as well as an ample store of jerked beef. The lost anchors presented a problem but this was solved by weighting some of the small anchors taken from Spanish prizes with 4-pounder cannon lashed to their shanks. On October 21st, ten days after her return, *Centurion* was ready for sea. The Spanish sergeant and his Indians waved a farewell from the bluff above the shore as she upped anchor and made sail. They were happy enough to be left behind with their now useless barque, and Anson had no qualms about leaving them; any day now a Spanish vessel from Guam would arrive to seek the reason for the non-appearance of their supply of meat.

"Goodbye to Tinian," said Midshipman Keppel, tugging at his black whiskers as he leaned across the after-rail to get a last view of the island. "In five weeks, maybe four, it'll be greetings to China. My word, Chips, we do see the world!"

"And the world sees you, remember," retorted Midshipman Carpenter, who was sporting a grass waistcoat woven for him by the Indians. "You'd better get that black bush off your face before you go ashore, or the Chinese girls will run away screaming."

159

"I'll make that an order, Mr Keppel." The Commodore had come up behind them unseen. "And you, Mr Carpenter, will oblige me by replacing that uncivilised garment with something better suited to a King's officer." His pale-blue eyes were twinkling and he grinned at their discomfiture. "I'm sure you would both wish the Chinese, whether male or female, to see in you the pattern of British naval officers. See to it."

"Aye, sir," they said in duet as he turned away.

"See that?" Carpenter whispered behind his hand. "George had a smile for us."

"Ye-es," said Keppel thoughtfully. "And he plays the flute in his cabin—I heard him last night when we were getting the last stores on board. Yes, Chips. George has changed."

5

"Land ho!" hailed the lookout in the foretop. "Right ahead, sir!"

"Shall I take a glass to the masthead, sir?" asked Peircy Brett.

"No, Mr Brett, thank you," said the Commodore. "I'll go myself."

He stepped down the ladder from the poop and walked for'ard along *Centurion*'s tilted deck. The ship was close-hauled under main and topsails, thrashing along with the spray flying over her beak-head. The strong wind from east of north, blowing for the past two days, had enabled her to hold the westward course he had set for Macao and to make steady progress, so that although it was only two days ago that they had sighted the Vele Rete Rocks off Formosa's southern tip, the landfall ahead must be the Chinese mainland. Anson did not doubt that landfall; his reckoning and Whipple's agreed precisely and he knew how carefully it had been checked. But he felt a need to see with his own eyes the coast that marked an important

160

stage in his new mission.

His glance as he walked took in a multitude of details: the new cordage of the main-shrouds; the ungainly fishing round the sprung foremast; Tully and half-a-dozen hands reeving a new set of tackles over the empty space where the lost longboat had once rested on the chocks. Through the ceaseless noises of wind and sea he could hear the dull clank of the pumps, which had never stopped since Tinian had been left astern twenty-three days ago; it had been fortunate that the leak in the bows had not become worse. There was much indeed to be done when *Centurion* came into Canton river, and he foresaw much negotiation before the Portuguese governor and the Chinese Viceroy at Canton would be persuaded to let him get the ship hove-down and afterwards completely refitted. For nothing less than that would do for the purpose he had in mind.

Under the bulwarks for'ard of the weather foremast-shrouds Pascoe Thomas was squatting with a book in his hand and a circle of boys round him. Anson recalled the first time he had noted the schoolmaster performing his educational duties as laid down in the recent Regulation—the only meritorious Regulation made by Admiralty in his lifetime, Anson believed—as *Centurion* took her departure from Ram Head. That had been more than two years ago, and the circle of boys had been a much more numerous one. He felt a sharp stab of pity at the thought of those youngsters dead from scurvy before they had begun to learn the meaning of life. As he swung himself into the shrouds he was reflecting that a man might reach the age of forty-five, as he had, before discovering the new meaning that life had for him.

He climbed easily to the foretop and pulled himself up beside the lookout, who knuckled his forehead respectfully and made room for him on the narrow platform. It was Purvis, Anson noted. He nodded curtly and took out his glass without a word; it would be interesting to see whether Purvis had learned his lesson. His glass showed him the distant coast at once, a level grey line on the rim of the grey-green sea. There were mountains in China, he had heard, but evidently they were not on this southern coast of the country. It was too early yet to ascertain whether he had made a good landfall, but so flat a coast at least suggested that the vast delta of the Canton river lay behind it with its thronged shipping which was sure to include some John Company ships; it was the East India Company that had developed the immense trade by which Macao, the Portuguese settlement at the mouth of the river, had become the chief port of south China. From the captains of the Indiamen he might get not only help in dealing with the neutral authorities of the port but also the first news of England he had had in over two years. It was remarkable how far away, in time as well as in space, England seemed now—and how different, in that remote world, the George Anson who had promised Kitty Clive that he would ask her to marry him when he returned.

A frown creased the Commodore's brow as he lowered his glass, but it vanished quickly. There were minor obstacles as well as great ones to be met and passed before he attained his objective, but he believed himself resolute enough to overcome them all. His eye fell on the lookout beside him dutifully scanning the arc of the horizon, and he remembered the first lieutenant's revised watch-bill and the suggestion Saumarez had made that morning.

"Yonder is the coast of China, Purvis," he said abruptly.

"Yes, sir." Purvis was equally brief.

"It may be a year or more before we reach England," Anson went on. "When we do so I shall procure your discharge. I assume that you will wish to return to your profession?"

"No, sir."

Anson frowned. "Indeed?"

"Not after this, sir," said Purvis, keeping his gaze on the sea.

"You'll not accept clean linen and good food in place of hardtack and a wet hammock? Speak up, man," added the

162

Commodore as the ex-tutor remained silent. "I'll not bite your head off."

"I don't like the life, sir," Purvis said slowly, "but I know I'd not be happy in any other. I'll sign on again." His eyes met Anson's for a moment. "I'd do that the more willingly, sir, if I knew I'd be serving under you—and so would every man on the lower deck."

For a breathing-space Anson could find nothing to say. He took refuge in a brusque change of subject.

"Mr Saumarez has recommended your advancement to bosun's mate. It has already received my ratification. Report to Mr Tully when your relief comes aloft."

"Aye, sir. Thank you, sir."

Purvis continued his scanning of the horizon. The Commodore climbed down the shrouds and went aft, too busy with his thoughts to take notice of the turning heads and questioning glances that attended his passing. Peircy Brett, who had the watch and was standing by the helm, looked eagerly at him for news but looked in vain. Only when the Commodore had taken half-a-dozen turns up and down his customary walk by the weather rail did he appear to realise that his officer-of-the-watch deserved enlightenment.

"A good landfall, Mr Brett, or so I believe," he said. And to the master, who crossed the deck to him, "The coast of the Canton delta, Mr Whipple. Keep her as she goes. And take the deck for ten minutes, if you please, while I confer with Mr Brett."

He went to his cabin under the poop-deck, the lieutenant following, and they sat down at the table. This was to be the last and briefest of many such conferences during the past three weeks; conferences à deux, for Anson had long decided that Saumarez would have neither Brett's sympathy for his ideas nor the imagination to add to them as Brett could do. It was one of the second lieutenant's notions that had been occupying the Commodore's attention when the masthead lookout interrupted their talk.

163

"If this wind holds," Anson said now, "we shall be anchored in Canton river before nightfall. And then both of us will have no more time to spend in planning the future of the Navy—for that, you know, is what we are about," he added with a smile. "I fancy their Lordships would call us mutineers, Peircy."

"Not if you achieve your purpose," Brett said seriously.

"No, for I would be a Lordship myself. But I've a long way to go before any of this"—Anson tapped a folio of papers that lay on the table—"can be even suggested. However, to the point. You were speaking just now of a uniform dress for Navy seamen."

Brett leaned forward eagerly. "And for naval officers too, sir. I don't think it's so trivial a matter as it may sound. You aim to make this a Navy that men will be proud to serve in—"

"Some are so today," Anson put in, thinking of Vokes and Purvis.

"Maybe. But how many seamen will volunteer for a King's ship? They know very well the conditions are devilish hard, far harder than they'd get in an Indiaman or even an East Coast collier."

"And the best that can be done won't greatly change them in our lifetime, Peircy."

"Perhaps not. But this could be a compensation, sir. Look at the Army," Brett hurried on enthusiastically. "Red coats, regimental facings, the panoply of Mars. The poor wretches live no better, and die as easily as the hands in a man-of-war, but they've something to show for it. The uniform dress tells the world they're King's soldiers, and they're proud to wear it."

"You'd play upon human vanity?" Anson said reflectively. "Well, it's a vice that's common to all men."

"And surely it's a deal better that a man should be attracted to volunteer, however it's managed, than that he should be cudgelled unconscious and flung on board a ship," Brett said.

The Commodore nodded slowly. "I believe you have

164

something of worth here, Peircy." He took up a quill and made a note on one of the papers in the folio. "This shall be added to our programme of—shall I say visions? You and I know—and I was recently told—that reform at the top is what is needed. That must come before any of the rest can follow."

"And you'll do it, sir," Brett cried. "You're the man to do it, my oath upon it."

"I hope to deserve your faith, my friend." Anson rose to his feet and went to stare out at the white-flecked seas. "But I need a mounting-block to get me on my high horse."

"You'll have it, sir, surely," said Brett, standing up. "Bring *Centurion* safely into Spithead, treasure and all, with your orders carried out in spite of disaster—it means promotion at the least."

"The mounting-block is not yet high enough," Anson said without looking round. "I need one thing more."

"May I ask what it is, sir?"

The Commodore turned with one of his rare smiles.

"You shall see, Peircy," he said.

SIX

The Galleon

1

His Majesty's ship *Centurion*, of sixty guns, shook herself free from the south-easterly rainstorm that had hung over her since she left the Macao anchorage and sped close-hauled into clearing weather. She was a very different ship from the leaky hulk that had reached that anchorage five months earlier. The 160-foot length of her hull glistened with new paint, black along the waterline below the lower-deck gunports and pale brown above, with chocolate-brown picking out the gunports. New gilding flashed on the scroll-work round her curved beak-head and along the galleries in her stern where there was now no sign of the damage wrought by the storms. She was under all sail to the topgallants, and as she came out from the fringe of the rain-squall a gleam of sunshine lit the dazzling new canvas that had replaced the dingy rags under which she had entered Canton river in November, and brightened the white cordage of standing and running rigging. These outward signs of her renovation, however, represented only a very small proportion of the work that had been done to fit her for the fourteen-thousand-mile voyage home to England.

Delays and deceptions, broken promises and plain rebuffs, had been Anson's experience for week after week and month after month when he attempted to get his ship refitted and replenished. The Portuguese Governor of Macao had proved to be useless for this end, being under the thumb of the Chinese Viceroy whose power in the vast Kwangtung province was absolute and who refused to consider the battered *Centurion* as a ship of the British Royal Navy. Patience and ingenuity won the day for the Commodore at last; a parade of a hundred seamen attired in the uniforms of the dead marines, a dinner-party on board for an inspecting Mandarin, the display of an armament which could destroy every vessel in Canton river without any risk to *Centurion*—these, with some carefully-placed bribes, gained a place for his ship in a dockyard where she could be careened. Everything had to be taken out of her (including her treasure, which was placed under strong guard) before the work could be commenced. Complete new sheathing of her bottom, caulking of deck and upper works, replacement of sprung masts and spars, and the vital repair to the big leak below the bowsprit, kept her in dock until early March. And after that she had to be provisioned and fully supplied with water and wood and repainted throughout. Not until April 19th was she once more at sea, heading southward for the Batavia passage and home.

Anson had sent Saunders back to England with his dispatches to Admiralty in a Swedish ship, and later an East Indiaman took home other officers of his company including Mitchell, Colonel Cracherode, and Walter the chaplain. As he had expected, he was able to get his first news of England from the Indiamen captains. One of them gave him a package of old newspapers, mostly *Gazettes*, and a paragraph in one of them informed him that Mr Handel's new oratorio *Messiah* had received its first triumphant performance. A footnote concerning some of the singers associated with Handel caught his eye; Mrs Cibber, remarked the critic, seemed likely to make as great a name for herself as the late lamented Mrs Clive.

So Kitty was dead. Anson, in the grip of the new purpose that possessed him, could feel only relief. Her passing removed the final obstacle to his plans, his parting promise to Kitty. Now he could close the book of his past life and begin the new one which was to hold so much more of real achievement.

The captains of the East India Company's ships rendered him more than one service, including help in amending *Centurion*'s shortage of men; he was able to add 27 prime seamen, Dutch and Lascars, to his crew, making a total of 227—just over half his proper complement. But not to those friendly captains, nor even to his own officers, did Anson so much as hint that he had any intention other than that of sailing southward, across the South China Sea and through the Java passage into the Indian Ocean, on his way to England. There was too much at stake. A word too many, and his unpredictable hosts might decide that as neutrals they ought to arrest him and his ship. So it was that when *Centurion* left Macao she had on board dispatches and letters for Batavia and introductions for the Commodore to notables in that thriving Dutch colony, though in fact Anson was not going anywhere near Batavia. She held her southerly course with difficulty, beating against the south-east Trades that blew in April, until she was out of sight of land. As she emerged into sunshine from under the dark curtain of rain Anson came out on the after-deck with Whipple the master at his side.

Like his ship, the Commodore had undergone a complete refit. His breeches and stockings were of white silk, his wide-skirted coat of wine-coloured satin. His triple-cocked hat was edged with gold lace, and the face beneath it was no longer hollow-cheeked but well filled-out and smoothly shaven. He halted by the helm and glanced quickly aloft and along the orderly decks. Saumarez (as smartly dressed as the Commodore) approached and touched his hat.

"I am going to put her about," Anson said. "Stand by sheets and braces, Mr Saumarez, if you please."

"Aye, sir."

The first lieutenant swung away and his shout brought the hands of the watch-on-deck leaping to their stations.

"Very well, Mr Whipple," said Anson.

"Aye, sir.—Helm up," Whipple told the quartermaster. "Larboard. Handsomely, now—meet her."

Centurion turned into and through the wind, her sails flapping and cracking as the sheets were released. She heeled steeply, then righted herself as the canvas filled on the starboard tack.

"Course nor'east a point east," said Whipple.

The Commodore turned and climbed to the poop-deck. The ship was steadying on her new course, the hands belaying and making fast along the weather and lee rails. He raised his voice.

"Mr Saumarez! I'll have all hands on deck. Muster them aft here."

He watched them come surging up from below, foremast hands, carpenters, cooks, boys, petty officers, the few marines; it was an orderly rush, and the mass of men that crowded into the small space afforded by the after-deck below the poop fell silent as soon as they had taken up position. He scanned the rows of faces upturned expectantly to him. Apart from a few newcomers he knew them all, and knew that with only half a crew *Centurion* was at this moment better manned than any ship in the Navy. At the rear of the crowd stood the little group of officers: Saumarez and Brett, Dennis, Keppel, Carpenter, and beyond them Pascoe Thomas and Ettrick the surgeon. He began to speak without preamble.

"We were heading south, for the Indian Ocean and home. Now we've altered course east, for the Pacific. I've had enough of the Pacific, and so have you, I'll warrant. But we've one more thing to do there before we go home—something we tried to do a year ago and failed. This time we're going to succeed. We're going to take the Acapulco galleon."

The irrepressible explosion of excited comment was stilled instantly by his uplifted hand. In the little pause before he continued speaking Anson felt a wave of unusual emotion pass over him: affection for these men

169

of his, men of every sort and origin—men of *Gloucester,*
Tryal, Anna, all *Centurion's* now—the sturdy remnant of
that famous Expedition of six ships to the South Sea and
his comrades through nearly three years of peril.

"The galleon sails each year for Manila, as you know,"
he went on. "Now Manila's but seven hundred miles as
the gull flies from our present position, and the galleon is
due to berth at Manila between the first and last days of
June. She won't berth this year, because *Centurion* will
intercept her as she comes in to make her landfall." Two
hundred pairs of eyes in brown faces were fixed eagerly
on him. "She is known to carry treasure worth a least a
quarter of a million English pounds. Add that to *Centu-*
rion's present treasure, calculate each man's share—and
you'll find there are riches enough for a lifetime of
luxury. And in taking this galleon from the Dons we shall
show 'em the mistake they made in challenging the Royal
Navy. Are you with me?"

A deafening shout was the instant response. Anson
quelled it before it could expand into the cheers which he
knew were bound to follow.

"This won't be as easy as the prizes we took off the Paita
coast, my lads," he told them. "This galleon's a big ship
and heavily armed. They say she carries five hundred
fighting-men or more—"

"A fig for 'em!" Here and there in the crowd a hothead
risked a shout. "Two to one—what's that? We've seen the
Spanish fight! Lay us alongside, sir, and—"

"*Still!*" thundered the Commodore, and the packed
mass froze into silence. "I've no time for your words. When
I want deeds I'll give my orders. Now mark this. It may be
two weeks or five before we fall in with the galleon. On
every day of those weeks there'll be drill—gun drill,
boat-drill, musketry practice—until every officer and man
knows his duty perfectly and can execute my orders on
the instant." He paused and sent his keen glance along
the close-packed ranks. "I've one thing more to say. You'll
have heard in Macao, as I have, that this Spanish ship has

170

sides so thick that no shot can pierce them. I'll believe that when I see a pig fly. And I mean to take *Centurion* so close that our twenty-four-pounder balls shall pass clean through her from side to side. Mr Saumarez, dismiss the hands, if you—"

The cheers broke loose then, cutting him short. The men yelled themselves hoarse for a full minute before officers and petty officers succeeded in sending down the watch below and clearing the after-deck, and Anson, turning away with a smile on his lips, affected not to notice the brief period of disorder. The smile was one of pleasure. He had deliberately roused his men's excitement and cupidity with a speech such as he had never made to them before, and doubtless some of their wild enthusiasm was due to the vaunting language he had used; but the cheering was for him, a mark of their confidence—and, perhaps, of their affection.' He remembered that nearly all these men had been under his command for three years. They had faced death and disaster because of his leadership, they had seen his mistakes and failures. And yet they still had confidence in him, eagerness to follow where he led. If anything was needed to strengthen Anson's resolution in the great undertaking he had set himself, he had it now.

2

"So, gentlemen, we have no occasion to move far from here," said the Commodore, setting his forefinger on the chart that was spread on the cabin table. "To make her landfall of Cape Espiritu Santo the galleon must come in from eastward and pass within sight of our lookouts."

"And it's mighty convenient indeed," remarked Dennis, "that the Dons are so regular in their habits."

"They have made the Manila voyage every year for a century and more," Anson said, rolling up the chart. "Every year at this time the treasure galleon has passed

171

through the chain of the Philippines by the San Bernardino passage, and we may be reasonably certain she will approach this year as usual."

The Commodore had summoned his three lieutenants to a council of war in the stern cabin. It was the morning of May 10th, and *Centurion* was moving lazily across a scarcely ruffled blue sea under topsails only, the faint breeze giving her only the slightest list to larboard. From outside the cabin came the occasional report of a musket; Corporal Thompson of the marines, acting as musketry instructor, had a small party of picked seamen improving their marksmanship by firing at a flask suspended from the foremast shrouds.

Anson had made the landfall of Formosa's southern tip on May 1st, and for the next week *Centurion* had sailed south-eastward well out of sight of the Luzon mainland, rarely logging more than 100 miles a day of southing because of adverse winds. He was early at the "rendezvous", for the information he had obtained—and there was little they did not know about the Acapulco galleon in the taverns and offices of Macao—showed that his intended prey never reached Manila before the last week in May. The Spaniards had by long experience learned to a nicety which weeks of the favourable season were most likely to provide fair winds and comfortable weather for the annual voyage, and it was their invariable custom to lay a course along the 12th parallel for the Philippine landfall of Cape Espiritu Santo. Since everyone but Anson himself had been certain that *Centurion* was sailing for England, no warning of his presence could have reached the Spaniards from Macao.

"Last time we met," Anson was saying, "we agreed on a plan for the operation of our guns." He had set the chart aside and now referred to a paper he had taken from his drawer. "I will recapitulate it for your comments. *Centurion* mounts twenty-four guns a side not counting bow and stern chasers. A broadside fully manned needs two hundred and forty men and my total crew is two hundred

172

and twenty-seven. But once a gun has fired and recoiled it can be sponged and reloaded by two men only. Therefore two men will be stationed at each gun for this duty, and there will be on each gun-deck four parties of ten men each who will move from gun to gun to run-out and fire the weapons as they are reloaded. I don't think we can better that."

"No, sir," Saumarez said, frowning, "but the method will need much practice if the hands aren't to fall over each other. There'll have to be a gunlayer with each party. And the space on the gun-decks—"

"All this is your affair, Mr Saumarez," interrupted Anson briskly. "I suggest you detail your gun-parties this afternoon and explain the procedure to them. The first practice can take place tomorrow in the forenoon watch. Mr Brett?"

Peircy Brett's square sun-reddened face was wrinkled in thought.

"It appears to me, sir," he said, "that the method robs us of one proven asset—the devastating effect of a whole broadside fired in unison."

"Ah, but there'll be an advantage to it ye've not thought of," put in Dennis. "Beg your pardon, sir," he added hastily to the Commodore.

"Say on, Mr Dennis. We shall need all the advantage we can get."

"Well, sir, I was hobnobbing with some ships' captains ashore in Macao who'd fought Spanish vessels often enough. Little better than pirates they were, I fear," said Dennis virtuously. "Anyhow, they all stuck to the same tale—that the Spanish gunners lie flat on the deck until the foe has discharged his broadside and then jump up and work their own guns while the enemy's reloading. That way the cowardly spalpeens dodge the shot."

"I would call them men of sense, Mr Dennis," Anson said with a smile. "But, as you say, our method will defeat their strategy. They can't dodge the shot from guns fired independently—unless, that is, they lie flat on the deck throughout the battle." He turned to the first lieutenant. "And on this point, Mr Saumarez, see to it, if you please, that all gunlayers take careful aim before they fire. There will be no firing until *Centurion* is within pistol-shot of the enemy and I want every shot to do the maximum damage possible."

"Aye, sir."

"Now as to the fighting-tops. I want as many men aloft as can be put there with room to load their muskets. How many will that give us, Mr Brett?"

"If we put the thirteen marines in the maintop, sir," said Brett, who had anticipated this question, "it's as many as it'll take. The handling of the ramrods takes a deal of space."

"Very well. Foretop and mizzen?"

"Mr Keppel and Mr Carpenter will be in charge there. Ten men all told in the foretop, and seven in the mizzen top—we can't put more there. And I'd suggest, sir, that there should be no more than three musketeers in each, the rest to have pistols. That would allow more elbow-room."

"Agreed. Thirty men in the tops, then. And whatever their weapon they must be the best small-arms marksmen in the crew. How are you dealing with their selection, Mr Dennis?"

Lieutenant Dennis, himself an excellent pistol-shot with three victorious duels on his record, had been put in charge of small-arms training. He answered without hesitation.

"Set aside the gunlayers and other men with special duties, sir, and I've four-score hands to choose from. The marines, of course, are all musket-men and they're practising daily. Corporal Thompson has fourteen seamen on the foredeck this minute—I picked the men who'd handled and fired musket or shotgun before—and he's testing them at target-practice."

Anson nodded. "By Mr Brett's plan you'll need six seamen musketeers and eleven pistol-men."

"Aye, sir—and I'll train the pistol-men myself."

"Very well. Impress on every man that his musket or pistol is to be aimed carefully at an individual target before he pulls trigger. There's to be no blazing away haphazard, and no firing from the tops until I give the signal."

The Commodore sat back in his chair and let his keen glance rest on each in turn of the three intent faces.

"You will see what I am attempting, gentlemen," he said. "An engagement at sea in which every operation of the fighting, on our side at least, shall be as effective as forethought and constant practice can make it. Inefficiency means wastage of lives as well as wastage of powder and shot." His eye met Brett's for an instant. "Inefficiency and lack of forethought—I say not where—have cost this Expedition some eighteen hundred lives in the three years that have passed. The men of *Centurion*'s present company have deserved to live. If my first purpose is to take this galleon and her treasure, my second is to do so with the least possible loss of life among my officers and men." He stood up. "Thank you, gentlemen. That is all."

Half-an-hour later Peircy Brett, having taken over the deck from Whipple who had stood-in for him while he was in council, was pacing up and down the weather side of the after-deck with an eye for the dark smudge of a rain-squall that hovered on the misty blue far to windward. Anson came out from the stern cabin and when they had exchanged salutes fell into step beside the second lieutenant. For a few minutes they paced up and down in silence. Then Anson spoke as if to himself.

"*Paciencia y barajar*—which is to say, patience, and shuffle the cards. But the hand is dealt and I must wait before I can play it. I find waiting the most difficult thing in the world, Peircy."

Brett showed his surprise. "I'd not have thought impatience was a fault of yours, sir."

"In this matter of the galleon, however, I am all impatience."

175

"This is the one thing more you needed, as you told me last year," Brett said.

"It's a thing I must have, Peircy." Anson took half-a-dozen steps without speaking. "What did you make of the news from England?" he asked abruptly. "The political news, I mean."

"Why, that Walpole won't last much longer, that when he goes there'll be war with France—is that what you mean, sir?"

"Yes. At home the end of old cabals and the formation of new. Abroad the emergence of the real enemy. For France is our great enemy of the future, Peircy, and you and I know that the struggle will in the end be resolved at sea. All will depend on that new Navy which we have talked of so often."

A grey shadow loomed above the weather rail and the ship gave a small lurch to leeward as the rain-squall struck her. The two men walked on, back and forth, with the silver drift of the rain enveloping them. Anson continued to speak, his beak of a nose thrusting through the driving moisture like the prow of a ship.

"That was our vision, Peircy, and this is now mine. *Centurion* comes home with the treasure of Acapulco and her mission completed. They'll promote me to Rear Admiral for certain. I shall press for a place on the Board of Admiralty, and with the Lord Chancellor at my back I can hardly fail to gain it when the old Board goes with the fall of Walpole. For First Lord I'll need time, and a good marriage to help me—"

He stopped short there. That phrase "a good marriage" had been in his mind more than once lately and he could not reconcile its implications with his remembrance of the Lady Elizabeth Yorke. He dismissed the idea with a gesture, sending a shower of drops flying from the heavily-brocaded sleeve of his coat. The squall was passing as swiftly as it had come, and his wet face glistened in pale sunshine as he turned with a smile to his companion.

"I was never wont to speak my thoughts aloud as I do

176

nowadays," he said. "It's perhaps because you're so good a listener, Peircy."

"I hope to do more than listen before long!" Brett cried earnestly, halting to face him. "I don't doubt you'll achieve your purpose, and you may count on my whole loyalty."

"I know it," Anson said quietly.

They resumed their pacing. After a moment the Commodore took his watch from its fob and glanced at it.

"Put her about at four bells of the afternoon watch, Mr Brett, if you please," he said formally. "And from this time forth it is a standing order that I'm to be called the instant any sail is sighted."

"Aye, sir," said Brett, and saluted as Anson turned to go aft to his cabin.

But there were few vessels in that vast empty space of sea east of the Philippines, and days passed into weeks without a single hail from the lookout at the masthead, regularly and monotonously relieved at every watch. *Centurion* sailed slowly on the short north-south patrol whose line stretched across the Acapulco galleon's approach route, with the coastline of the Philippines a league beyond her western horizon. Fair weather with intervals of rain and light squalls made small demand on the seamanship of her company and at the end of three weeks the frequent drills and mock alarms had begun to pall. Lieutenant Peter Dennis, who had begun to keep a journal, made this entry:

May 31. Exercising our men at their quarters, in great expectation of meeting with the galeons very soon, this being the eleventh of June, their stile.

Dennis, in the course of the endless discussions in the wardroom, had become the champion of a theory that the Spaniards would send two galleons on the annual voyage this year, the voyage of 1742 having been prevented by Anson's presence off Acapulco. It was significant that the possibility of having to fight two enemy ships instead of

177

one made no difference to the eagerness of *Centurion*'s crew. But the "great expectation" began to fade into disappointment as the first week of June passed without incident into the second, and Anson and his lieutenants were kept busy devising means for keeping their men on tiptoe. Prizes for marksmanship with musket or pistol, for speed of loading, for the first team into the fighting-tops, did something towards this, and by way of diversion there were occasional hornpipe competitions on the foredeck to the squeaky music of Seaman Fortune's fiddle. At least the long interval of waiting enabled the Commodore to perfect to the last detail his plans for action and the several alternatives which the weather or the tactics of the enemy ship might force upon him. Every individual man knew precisely what would be required of him in any possible event. Outnumbered as he was sure to be, Anson had no intention of boarding the Spaniard except in the last resort, yet a boarding-party was selected and exercised in its mustering and boat-drill as assiduously as if its use was a certainty. As for the gunners, the 24-pounders on main and upper decks set the ship a-tremble daily as the trucks were hauled rumbling up to the gunports in practice, while the teams that trotted from gun to gun could have done their work blindfold.

The twentieth day of June dawned dark and overcast, with the purple-grey shadows of rain-squalls drifting across a ruffled green sea. At two bells in the morning watch the masthead lookout hailed the deck. And that seagull-screech was music to the ears of *Centurion*'s men.

"Sail-ho, dead to wind'ard! Distant eighteen mile! Three-master, ship-rigged!"

This could only be the Acapulco galleon.

3

In the misty circle of Peircy Brett's glass the galleon looked enormous though she was only now hull-up from

178

the deck. A fitful breeze was blowing isolated rainstorms across the ruffled dark-blue and she vanished behind a screen of rain for half-a-minute; when she reappeared Brett saw that her topgallant sails were being taken in. That made it certain that she had recognised *Centurion* as an enemy and intended to fight. A joyful shouting from the hands crowding the foredeck showed that the galleon's action had been perceived there. Ten minutes had passed since eight bells of the morning watch had been sounded and the watch below, having breakfasted, had come on deck to relieve their shipmates, but the second lieutenant (who had the forenoon watch) perceived that not a man of those who had been on duty had left the deck. He raised his voice in a stentorian bellow.

"Starboard watch, there! Get below, d'ye hear? Twenty minutes for breakfast."

No King's ship went into action without first feeding the crew, if that was possible. The foredeck cleared, leaving only the men of the larboard watch. Brett glanced aft to where the Commodore stood on the highest point of the poop-deck with his glass to his eye. With these light airs and the consequent slow rate at which the two ships were closing it would be another two hours before they could engage.

"Mr Brett! I'll have the spritsail yard rigged and the sail hoisted, if you please," Anson called down to him.

"Aye, sir."

As Brett gave the necessary orders that set the hands jumping to perform this task he wondered a little at the order; the spritsail would give little or no extra way with the present wind and its purpose was to enable *Centurion* to lie alongside if necessary with the intention of boarding. When he focused his glass on the Spaniard again he allowed himself an inward chuckle of amusement. The enemy ship had already rigged her spritsail and Anson had simply replied to the challenge with a counter-challenge—like fighting-cocks crowing at each other before the conflict, Brett thought.

Saumarez came across the deck to him, wiping his mouth after a breakfast of coffee and biscuit. His dark face was alive with anticipation.

"She's game, it seems," he commented, staring at the distant galleon. "Whistle for a wind, Mr Brett—at this rate we'll not be able to congratulate each other before nightfall."

"I trust it'll be earlier than that—*sir*," Brett replied.

They grinned at each other. The Commodore had let it be understood that in the event of the galleon being taken Saumarez would be promoted captain into her (she being commissioned as a ship in His Majesty's Service) with Brett receiving permanent promotion to first lieutenant of *Centurion*. Meanwhile, Brett would command the upper-deck guns in the coming fight, with Dennis in charge of the main deck.

The two officers resumed their observation of the enemy, though for the moment there was little enough to see. With the fickle breeze puffing intermittently on her quarter the galleon was steering to intercept the British ship, who was close-hauled under plain sail, but between them they were closing at little more than two knots. As a prelude to battle, Brett reflected, this was singularly peaceful; the smooth and almost imperceptible motion, the intermittent murmur of conversation from the watch grouped along the weather rail, the rustle of the light wind in the canvas and the lazy creaking of spars and blocks—these were the background sounds of a calm morning at sea in time of peace. The vessel far away to windward, a mere dot in the immensity of the dark sea, looked too insignificant to hold anything of menace. A seaman came aft to the belfry abaft the helm and rang two double strokes; four bells of the forenoon watch.

The Commodore had come down from the poop-deck to confer with Whipple, who was standing beside the quartermaster. Now he came across the deck with the master, acknowledging the salutes of the two lieutenants as he approached. His face, Brett saw, wore that look of

180

fixed placidity which in the past three years he had come to associate with the imminence of peril.

"Two hours before we engage, gentlemen," he remarked. "That is, unless the wind freshens."

Saumarez glanced up at the hazy overcast and sniffed the air. "Small likelihood of that, sir. All the same, the Don has the weather-gage."

"He may keep it. There can be no manoeuvring in light airs such as these. What distance away do you make her, Mr Whipple?"

"Four miles, sir, I'd say," said the master.

"Three's nearer the mark," the first lieutenant amended; he put his glass to his eye. "Hallo! They're clearing for action. Must've had a deal of deck cargo, because there's all manner of lumber going overboard. Cattle too, by God! The damned villains, tossing the poor beasts overside to drown!"

"And yet, Mr Saumarez," Anson said mildly, "you would be delighted to see five hundred men of Spain blown overside if a lucky shot found her magazine."

"Aye, sir—but while *Centurion* had a boat left to pick 'em up we'd not be letting Davy Jones get his claws on them.—Up go her colours, sir, Spanish flag at the ensign staff and royal standard of Spain at main-topgallant masthead."

As he spoke the report of a cannon came clearly on the wind as the galleon fired a formal gun to leeward. Anson nodded approvingly.

"I begin to like this Spanish captain," he said. " 'The glass of fashion, and the mould of form.' We had better show ourselves willing to meet him. I'll have main courses and topgallants off her, Mr Saumarez, if you please. All hands—we don't want her to know our deficit."

At Saumarez's shouted orders the bosuns' calls shrilled and a torrent of men poured on deck and up the shrouds. As if by magic the big courses and lesser upper sails disappeared from the yards and *Centurion*'s three masts wore only the topsails. The Commodore waited until the sheets were hauled close and made fast and then gave the order to beat to quarters. The stirring *rafale* of the marines' drums (how long ago, thought Brett, since they had sounded at Paita!) brought another orderly rush, this time directed mainly along the gun-decks but with a triple file of men ascending the shrouds to gain the square platforms of the fighting-tops at the head of main, fore, and mizzen masts. The red coats of the marines mounted to the maintop and Corporal Thompson's bull roar could be heard admonishing a comrade to keep his bloody musket to himself. Then the multitudinous footfalls ceased, the voices fell silent, and all was as quiet as before. The galleon, now two miles or so ahead, came slowly round, bringing-to with her bows to the wind and her lofty stern with its huge poop lantern towards *Centurion*. Creeping close-hauled across the scarcely-rippled water, the English ship closed minute by minute the gap between them. The leeway she was making would bring her on the Spaniard's larboard beam. Anson spoke from the poop-deck.

"Mr Brett, I'll have all guns loaded. The starboard guns only to be run out."

Brett ran for'ard to shout his orders to main and upper deck, but so quiet was the ship that he might have given them from his stance on the after-deck. *Centurion* vibrated to the rumble of the gun-trucks, and the curt shouts of the gunners reporting their pieces loaded and run-out ceased as the thunder of the trucks stopped. Into the ensuing silence dropped the four double strokes of the ship's bell marking noon. A grey squall of rain blew across, hiding the galleon, and when it cleared she was seen to be still hove-to and barely half-a-mile distant.

"Hoist the battle ensign and my pendant, Mr Saumarez."

Brett could see confused activity on the Spaniard's upper deck; they were still hurling miscellaneous lumber overboard in a last-minute attempt to give themselves more fighting room. The Commodore had observed it.

His quiet voice carried right for'ard to where Mr Cargill the gunner waited expectantly.

"Bow chaser, Mr Cargill. Open fire."

The first shot of the battle, a purely harassing one, did no more than lodge itself in the galleon's quarter-gallery but it served its purpose of causing confusion on her deck. The bow chaser fired again, without apparent effect. But now *Centurion* was close on the enemy's quarter and less than half-a-mile from her, and the Spaniard's after-guns began to fire as soon as they could be traversed to cover her. Brett heard the high-pitched screech of a ball and multiple *twang!* as half the mizzen-shrouds on the lee side parted.

"Mr Tully! Reeve and splice here."

The bosun's little party ran to obey, while the irregular explosions, with their accompanying jets of smoke and flame, intensified as *Centurion* came gradually beam-and-beam with the galleon. A shock and a shudder, twice repeated, told that the Spanish balls were striking home, and from her tops came the flash and crackle of musketry. Involuntarily Brett swung round to look up at the Commodore. The bow chaser had ceased fire and not another shot had replied to the enemy guns. Anson held in his hand the silver whistle that was slung on a lanyard round his neck. He spoke quietly to the helmsman below him.

"Bring her closer to the wind. Hold her so."

In the foretop Midshipman Keppel crouched pistol in hand beside his nine marksmen. Peering above the bulwark that surrounded the top he could see the men in the Spaniard's maintop through the smoke of their firing. They were very slowly moving astern as *Centurion* glided forward and they were less than a hundred and twenty feet from him. A bullet thudded into the foot of the topmast behind him, where a seaman lay groaning with a musket-shot through his shoulder. Why, why didn't the signal come?

The long clear peal of Anson's whistle pierced the noise

of small-arms and cannon fire.

"Up!" shouted Keppel, scrambling to his feet. "Her foretop's your target—aim—fire!"

He heard the thunder of *Centurion*'s guns below him as his pistol banged in unison with a volley that came near to deafening him. The galleon's foretop was nearly opposite now and at forty yards' range muskets and pistols made deadly practice. Amid screeches and yells men pitched headlong to the Spaniard's deck or hung limply across the bulwark of her top. Keppel's gaze fixed itself fascinatedly on a wounded man who had fallen into the boarding-netting that had been rigged along the galleon's rail and lay writhing there like a trodden worm. He pulled himself together.

"Muskets reload! Pistols, aim at the officers!"

That had been the Commodore's order: first volley at the tops, second at the deck. From main and mizzen the hail of lead flew simultaneously with the fire from the foretop. On the crowded deck of the galleon the officers were conspicuous in their gold-laced hats and brocaded coats, easy targets for muskets firing from overhead at forty paces. Every shot of the marines in the maintop took effect. But the Spanish broadside was fully engaged now, the billowing smoke with its nucleus of spurting orange flames filling the space between the two ships. *Centurion*'s guns roared from upper and main decks as the trained teams raced from gun to gun to throw their weight on the tackles and run the reloaded cannons up to the gunports, the ceaseless rumble of the trucks adding its lesser note to the deafening orchestra of 24-pounders and musketry. Splinters flew from rail and deck of the English ship and a ball ploughed through one of the ten-man teams on the upper deck, smashing one man into bloody rags and wounding two others. The shot from both her gun-decks was pounding the Spaniard's hull between wind and water.

"Mr Brett!" The Commodore, hands behind back, had crossed the deck to where the lieutenant was standing abaft the mizzen. "I'll have the quoins of the upper-deck guns out, if you please."

"Aye, sir."

Brett dashed along the guns, dodging the hurrying teams, to give his order. With the quoins removed the twelve guns hurled their balls at higher elevation, wreaking havoc on the galleon's crowded deck and sending the splinters flying from masts and spars. Relentlessly the lower-deck guns hammered away at the huge red-brown hull intermittently visible through the drifting smoke.

Very slowly *Centurion* was over-reaching on her opponent, her poop-deck drawing opposite the galleon's mainmast. Brett, turning to see what the Commodore would make of this, saw a white furrow score itself across the deck six feet from Anson as he moved towards the helm, the shot ricocheting to fly through the larboard rail in a shower of splinters. Anson walked on without pausing in his leisured stride.

"Starboard helm, quartermaster. Steady as you go."

There was scarcely enough wind to influence *Centurion*'s course, but slowly she answered the rudder and turned until she lay with her broadside fronting the galleon's larboard bow. The cannon thundered on, while only the for'ard Spanish guns could now traverse sufficiently to hit the English ship. Down came the Spaniard's mizzen yard in a tangle of cordage. The huge ensign at her stern leapt in the air and fell with its gaudy red-and-yellow draped across the poop rail and smouldering into flame. An officer, splendidly dressed in a yellow coat with heavy gold aiguillettes, dashed along the poop to gather in the burning folds and smother the flames. Brett heard Anson's voice raised to its full volume for the first time.

"Musketeers! Cease fire!"

The order came just too late. A shot from *Centurion*'s maintop struck the yellow-coated officer and he spun round and fell from sight. An instant after Peircy Brett witnessed this incident, the starboard rail a few paces from him seemed to explode with a noise like a thunder-

185

clap and something struck him with fearful force on the side of the head.

Brett came back to consciousness and pain in his own cabin, where he had been carried and placed on his cot. The bandaging that swathed his head allowed only one eye to scan his surroundings, and this restricted vision showed him the large red face of Pascoe Thomas the schoolmaster regarding him earnestly. A sense of something lacking troubled him for a moment, until he realised that it was quiet in the cabin; the sounds of battle had ceased.

"*Salus ex victoria*, Mr Brett," said Thomas, perceiving his recovery. "I speak thus by way of reassurance, since you've lain insensible a full half-hour."

"The galleon struck, then?" Brett mumbled through his bandages.

"*Nuestra Señora de Cobadonga*"—Thomas rolled out the name unctuously—"hauled down her colours an instant after you were smitten down by a billet of wood the size of my arm. You've half-a-dozen stitches in your scalp but no fractured bone, if the surgeon's to be trusted."

Brett struggled with the agonising throbs of pain that made it difficult to think. "And our losses?"

"Remarkable, quite remarkable," said Thomas, who was plainly anxious to talk. "I've but now come from transcribing the reports for the Commodore. We have two seamen killed and sixteen wounded, none seriously. The Spaniards lost sixty-seven killed—and all her officers but one—and above ninety wounded. Mr Saumarez has four hundred and ninety prisoners on his hands."

Saumarez would be on board the *Cobadonga* in command, Brett remembered.

"I should be on deck," he said, attempting to sit up.

The schoolmaster restrained him. "You'll please to stay where you are, Mr Brett, until Ettrick gives the word," he said firmly. "We're hove-to and can manage without a first lieutenant until repairs are completed to both ships. The Commodore is in charge, and he's worth any three lieutenants as you're well aware."

Brett nodded emphatically and wished he hadn't.

"A quite remarkable man," Thomas pursued with enthusiasm. "I was on deck throughout the action, Mr Brett, and I may say the Commodore's calmness of behaviour affected me so strongly that I was calm myself. There is a certain greatness in the man, sir, and that I will maintain.—But I neglect my duty." He picked up a beaker of liquid from beside him. "The medicaster Ettrick required me to see that you drank this. It is, I believe, a sleeping-draught."

With the schoolmaster's arm supporting his shoulders, Brett contrived to insinuate the rim of the beaker between the folds of bandage and drain the contents.

"Let us hope it proves efficacious," said Thomas sceptically, setting down the empty vessel.

Brett found himself able to grin. "You would prefer it to have been lime-juice?" he suggested.

"A matter not to be jested upon, sir," said Pascoe Thomas severely. "Be the sum of our treasure what it may, its value is not be compared with the remedy we have discovered on this voyage. When my journal is published in England—"

He stopped abruptly and stood up, crouching under the deck beams, as the Commodore ducked into the cabin. There being no room for three men in that tiny space, Thomas removed himself and Anson sat on the stool he had occupied. He reached out a hand and placed it for a moment on the lieutenant's shoulder.

"How is it with you, Peircy?"

"Well enough, sir. An hour's sleep and I'll be fit for duty."

"We shall see about that. Thomas has told you of our victory?"

"Yes, sir. Pray accept my most sincere felicitations upon it." Brett remembered the hammering of the Spanish broadsides. "Is the ship much damaged?"

"Fifteen shot through her hull," said Anson, "but none

187

that can't be plugged. *Centurion's Prize*—it's thus I've named Mr Saumarez's command—has a hundred and fifty shot-holes between wind and water, and her masts and rigging are badly cut about. We may do something for her at Macao but I doubt whether she will ever reach England."

The throbbing in Brett's skull was lessening its pain and he felt his senses leaving him.

"But you have—all that you want, sir, now," he muttered with an effort.

"Yes, Peircy. My thanks to you for that, and to all *Centurion*'s company. What use I make of my gains time will show."

To Peircy Brett the Commodore's voice had become an unintelligible murmur. He was dimly aware of Anson leaving the cabin and of a silvery chime that ushered him into oblivion—six bells of the afternoon watch.

4

Through the white veils of mist that lay across the waters of Spithead a great ship moved steadily under plain sail. The early sunlight of a June morning dazzled and darkened on her white canvas and the white gulls that wheeled and screamed above her mastheads as she passed in and out of the vapour-wreaths. This was the last sea-mile of a voyage that had lasted for three years and nine months and taken her clear round the world. *Centurion* was coming home.

Commodore Anson stood with his hands on the taffrail of the poop-deck, his gaze fixed on the insubstantial mists. Soon she would bring Gilkicker Point on her larboard bow, he was thinking, and that would be the end of a voyage as long, and as beset by hazards, as any ever made by a King's ship. He was glad that *Centurion* was alone on this final stretch up the Channel and in past the Island. Pleasant as it would have been to reach Portsmouth in company with the great Spanish treasure-ship he had captured, it was more satisfactory to enter harbour in the one ship that had not failed him on his long mission, the ship that had come to seem almost a part of himself.

The Spanish prisoners taken in the *Cobadonga* had been placed under the care of the Chinese Viceroy at Canton, who had friendly trading relations with Spain. But the galleon had proved to be beyond repair and had been sold. Her treasure, consisting of 1,313,843 pieces of eight and 35,682 ounces of virgin silver, was stowed in *Centurion's* hold; with the booty taken from Paita and the vessels captured on the Pacific coast, this gave a cargo worth some two million pounds sterling for Anson to land at Portsmouth. The lion's share of this, after Treasury and Admiralty had taken their toll, would go to Anson, with fortunes for his officers according to rank, but every man on board would have more than sufficient to "set him up as a gentleman" for life.

To Anson the money was another means to his end. Wealth, prestige, promotion in his Service—these formed the solid mounting-block for the bestriding of his high horse (as he had phrased it to Peircy Brett) on which, once mounted, he would set lance in rest against the political jobbery and double-dealing that ensnared the Royal Navy. The power he coveted was almost in his grasp. The voyage was nearing its triumphant conclusion. And yet, as he stood on his poop-deck at seven in the morning of June 15th 1744, Anson was filled with sadness. Whatever his new future held it could not include command of *Centurion*. And for her he felt a deep affection such as he had never felt for a woman—indeed, he told himself, there never was a woman who possessed the staunchness and spirit of this ship of his. It was strange, perhaps, that as the thought crossed his mind he had a transient vision of Elizabeth Yorke's oddly attractive face and dark intelligent eyes. It faded as a gap in the mist to larboard revealed the grey stones of Gilkicker Fort a mile away on the bow.

"Mr Cargill!"

Down on the upper deck the gunner doffed his hat and turned to shout an order to the waiting gun-crews. The first gun of the fort's salute boomed and was answered by the flame and crash of *Centurion*'s cannon. Eleven guns for his Commodore's pendant; there would be thirteen for the Rear-Admiral's flag that might soon be his. And then he could throw himself into the work he had set himself, the work that was needed now more urgently than ever. For yesterday off the Start he had learned from a schooner captain that England was at war with France.

"Sir!" The first lieutenant's voice came from the deck below. "Permission to take in sail."

"Do so, Mr Brett, if you please."

The hands raced aloft to take in the main courses. Every man fit and lively; Pascoe Thomas's insistence on regular doses of lime-juice might well have something to do with the absence of scurvy on this long voyage from China. That should not be forgotten in the future. But close at hand now were the fresh meat and good ale of old England—and there on the beam, glimpsed through the parting mists, was the emerald-green slope of Gilkicker Down. He made out the figures of two or three people there, and horses too, before *Centurion* passed the angle of the fort and the green slope slid out of sight. Home. Home and the ending of a long adventure for his ship's company. But for him, George Anson, this was not an ending but a beginning.

Epilogue, December 1744

The little red-faced man in the shabby scarlet coat stared suspiciously at the fine gentleman who bowed before him in wine-coloured satin.

"Eh?" he barked. "What?"

The Duke of Bedford bent to whisper again in the little man's ear. "Rear-Admiral George Anson, your Majesty," he said. "Newly appointed to the Board of Admiralty."

"Hah!" exclaimed King George, so loudly that the brilliant company gathered in the reception room interrupted its low-voiced chatter for a moment. "The voyage and the treasure. *Herrlich! Heldenmütig!*" He held out a pudgy hand and Anson bent over it. "No, no! The shake-hand, sir!"

"Your Majesty is too kind," said Anson.

"Between the admiral and the soldier, the shake-hand," declared the King. "This coat, Admiral, I wore at Dettingen. I led the English army into battle. The French ran. Now they shall run from our ships, *hein?*"

"I trust so, your Majesty."

"It must be so. You shall see to it, Admiral." The King sank his voice to a hoarse whisper. "The old Board is gone, with that damned Walpole. Bedford here has the Administration and he tells me you are sworn to put things to rights. Make me a Royal Navy, Admiral, that shall beat the French whenever it meets them."

Anson met the stare of the protuberant blue eyes

191

steadily. "I shall use my utmost endeavours, your Majesty, to give our English seamen the Fleet they deserve," he said.

"*Gut, gut.*" King George patted the Admiral's arm. "Depend upon my help, depend upon my help. You are married?" he added abruptly.

"No, your Majesty."

"You should be married. My late dear wife—" The King brushed away a genuine tear. "I never knew a woman fit to buckle her shoe. Get married, Admiral, get married."

"I shall fulfil your Majesty's wishes as soon as possible," said Anson, and meant it.

The King nodded and turned to speak to the Duke of Bedford. Anson bowed himself away until ceremony permitted him to send a questing glance along the ranks of ladies and gentlemen standing or sitting under the light of the glittering chandeliers. Lord Hardwicke's massive form was easily discerned. In the chair beside which the Lord Chancellor was standing sat a girl in a white gown. Anson went towards her with quick strides, conscious that he was smiling with pleasure at the encounter. Elizabeth Yorke's quaint features were transfigured by her answering smile as he approached. And Anson, seeing the light in her eyes, knew that it would shine upon his endeavours throughout the strenuous years to come.